HOT MESS EXPRESS

Sibby Series Book V

E. SLATE

Tabula Rasa Publishing

To the end of an era.

Disclaimer

No gators were injured during the writing of this book.

Chapter 1

"You will never defeat me, heathen!" I yelled.

Sophie brandished her mock sword. "The kingdom will never be yours! I will never surrender!"

"En guard!" I pulled my own matching rapier from its sheath at my waist and posed to attack.

Sophie lunged for me, our wooden blades clacking against one another.

"You, evil queen, have done your last dirty deed!"

I held back a grin.

We whirled and twisted, fencing and dueling. She charged.

I feigned to the left.

"Mom, you were supposed to die," she admonished.

"Oops. Sorry. Go again?"

She nodded. Sophie lunged once more, her mock sword sliding between my armpit and my side. I dropped my rapier and collapsed to my knees.

"You have struck me," I moaned. "The better queen has won."

I dramatically fell onto my back and began to twitch, pretending I was dying the most horrible of deaths.

Through half-mast lids, I watched Sophie creep closer. When she was within arm's reach, I grabbed her and pulled her down to the ground and began to tickle her.

Her peals of laughter rang through the backyard.

"No fair," she gasped when I ceased my ticklish attack.

"All's fair in true love and make believe, kiddo," I teased. "How was my death?"

"Ten out of ten, two thumbs up."

We sat next to each other, cross-legged on the lawn. She leaned her head against my shoulder. "You're the best mom ever."

"How do you know?" I asked. "You've only had one mom."

"I know," she informed me, in her lofty seven-year-old worldly voice.

The back door slid open, and Jasper ran out to greet us, his entire butt wagging in happiness to see us. Aidan came out behind him.

The dog went to Sophie first, bathing her face with his tongue. Laughing, she pushed him away. Jasper came to me next and flopped down onto his back. I rubbed his belly for a few moments, and when he'd had enough, he bounded over to Aidan.

The man looked positively delectable in a pair of ratty khaki shorts, an old gray T-shirt, and a backwards Mets cap.

Jeepers, he was hot.

"Who won the sword fight?" he asked.

"Sophie, of course," I said. "She puts Arya Stark to shame. I didn't stand a chance."

"Who's Arya Stark?" Sophie asked.

"A character who's an expert with the sword," I told her.

My daughter had gone as Robin Hood last year for Halloween and even after she'd physically outgrown the costume, she hadn't been willing to let it go. So, I'd sewn her a new one, with room to grow.

She wore the costume four days a week, at least. And when she wasn't in her Robin Hood costume, she preferred overalls.

"Where's Ollie?" Aidan asked.

"Upstairs, making sure he's packed everything."

Aidan walked to me and reached down to help me off the grass. He then began brushing off my backside.

"I think I'm good," I said in amusement.

"Nah, you're covered in dirt," he said with a wink.

I arched a brow.

"Soph, why don't you go and tell Oliver that your grandparents are on their way," Aidan said.

"M'kay," she said, running toward the house, black braids flying behind her head. Jasper trotted after her.

"Seriously? I can't still be dirty," I said to Aidan.

"You're Sibby. You're always dirty."

"You made that sound sexual."

He pulled me into his arms and stared down at me. "Hello."

"Hello."

Aidan kissed me.

"You know you look like a college frat guy with the backwards cap, don't you?"

"Oh, definitely." He smiled, making his dimples pop up and say hello.

"God, were you this hot when we met?"

"Yes, I was irresistible even then."

"It was the flannel shirt," I assured him. "The dimples were just the icing on the lumbersnack cake."

We headed into the house which was nothing short of a wreck. I winced. "Yikes. I forgot that we destroyed this place last night."

"Don't look at it," Aidan suggested. "When the kids leave, we'll divide and conquer the clean-up."

"Or we could keep the living room fort we made with the kids and watch cartoons," I suggested. "And eat ice cream for dinner."

"We did that with the kids last night," he reminded me. He lifted his T-shirt to show off a six pack. "If I want to keep this and not have a dad bod, then ice cream for dinner two nights in a row isn't the best idea."

I reached around and grabbed my *tuchus*. "Probably right. But it's a hell of a lot of fun. I do suppose we could increase our cardio workout."

"We could."

"I was referring to sex."

He laughed. "Yeah, I gathered as much. And I fully support that endeavor."

"Excellent. Glad to have you aboard, sailor." I saluted him and then with a sigh, I went to the sink and began loading the dishes into the dishwasher.

The twins came down the stairs, arguing. "Ollie, please," Sophie begged.

"No," he said. "I don't want to."

She'd changed out of her costume and put on a pair of her favorite overalls. She pushed back a curl that had escaped one of her braids and glared at her brother.

They were best friends and worst enemies. And so completely different.

Oliver was currently wearing a clip-on red bowtie and a pair of Chinos. His dark hair was parted and combed.

He was as serious as an accountant during tax season. Looked like one too. I had to stop myself from squeezing the stuffing out of him because he was so cute.

"What's going on?" Aidan asked as he went to the fridge.

"I asked Ollie if he'd be the Sheriff of Nottingham to my Robin Hood while we're on our road trip, and he said he wouldn't."

"Then that's his choice," I said.

Aidan tossed me a loaf of bread. "Grilled cheese?"

"Heck yes," I said. "Oh, I guess we're standing firm at not eating like garbage?"

"It's gourmet cheese," he said. "From France. It makes a difference."

I wrinkled my nose at him.

"Can I have a tomato on mine?" Ollie asked.

"Absolutely." I pulled out a cutting board and washed a beefsteak tomato that Annie had grown in her garden.

I made two extra sandwiches in case Bud and Nancy hadn't eaten lunch and left them on the counter.

Sophie finished her sandwich first, all but inhaling it like a wolverine. She got up from the table and brought her plate to the dishwasher.

"Can I wait out front for Grandma and Grandpa?" she asked.

"Let's all go," Aidan suggested, polishing off the last bite of his sandwich.

The four of us went out front. Oliver sat on the porch swing with Sophie, but Sophie couldn't sit still. She launched herself off the swing and decided to do cartwheels across the front lawn.

"Hey, Soph, maybe give your belly some time to digest," Aidan said.

"Rats," she muttered, plopping down onto the grass. She tilted her face up to the sunshine.

"I'll have to count your new freckles when you get home in a few weeks," I said.

"I hope my face is covered in them," she said.

"You need to wear sunscreen," Oliver informed her. "You don't want to burn."

She stuck her tongue out at her brother and he returned in kind.

"Let's go over the rules again for when you're in a national park," I said looking from Sophie to Oliver and then back to her.

"No feeding the animals," she recited. "No touching the animals. No wandering near smelly water. Listen to Grandma and Grandpa."

I grinned. "Yup. You got it."

Sophie flipped her body around and did a head stand. "I'm going to miss you so much!"

"Sophie," I warned. "Do I need to clean out your ears? Your father said you need time to digest."

She lowered her legs to the ground.

"I like it when you're stern," Aidan whispered.

"Hush."

"Are you going to miss me?" Sophie asked me.

"Absolutely."

"Are you going to miss Ollie?" she inquired.

"Without a doubt. I'm so jealous you get to go to Yellowstone and see Old Faithful. It's going to be lonely around here without you guys."

"But you've got Dad to keep you company," Oliver pointed out.

I looked at my husband, who was lookin' at me like he couldn't wait to chase me naked around the kitchen.

"Too true." I glanced at Oliver. "You sure you don't want to change? Aren't you hot?"

He shook his head.

I tried another avenue. "You're going to be sitting for a long time. You don't want to wrinkle your clothes."

"I want to look nice for Grandma and Grandpa," he said.

"Well, you look very handsome," I commented.

"Just like his father, right?" Aidan asked.

"Right."

Bud and Nancy would be here any minute to scoop up the kids and then they were gone for six weeks on an epic road trip adventure.

Six weeks during the summer, and for the first time in a long while Aidan and I would be kid free.

Aidan's phone chimed with a text. He checked the screen. "They're turning onto our street."

"They're coming!" Sophie shrieked and then hopped up.

A few minutes later, Bud and Nancy parked a giant motorhome at the curb.

"That thing is a beast," Aidan muttered.

"Not a beast. A tank. I don't remember it looking that big," I said.

"That's what she said," he quipped.

"We're still saying that? After all these years?"

"I don't think it'll ever go out of style."

Bud cut the engine of the motorhome and then he and Nancy climbed out.

"Grandpa!" Sophie screamed as she ran to her grandfather. She wrapped her arms around his legs and he pretended she almost knocked him over.

"What? No Robin Hood costume?" he asked.

"I packed it."

Bud tugged on her left braid and then looked at his grandson. He held out his hand to him. "You're a mighty smart dresser, Oliver."

Oliver beamed and took his hand, giving it a hearty shake. "Thanks, Grandpa."

"Let's load up your suitcases," Bud said. "We've got a long way to go."

"Are you guys hungry?" I asked. "We made grilled cheese sandwiches for you."

"Sounds good, thanks," Bud said.

Nancy placed her hands on her hips and pretended to be upset. "Don't I get a hug and a kiss?"

"Hey, Mom," Aidan said with a grin.

"Don't *hey mom* me." She embraced her son and then stepped back to look at him. "You look tired."

"Mom." Aidan rolled his eyes.

"Are you sleeping enough? Eating enough? Or are you and Caleb burning the candle at both ends?"

"Have to make sure everything is ready to go for the craft brew festival," Aidan said.

Nancy's gaze slid to me. "And you?"

"And me what?" I asked.

"When am I getting another romance novel from you?"

I groaned. "You sound like my agent. Her emails have been in all caps lately. I'll tell you what I told her. I'm enjoying writing children's books under a pen name, but when I have a stellar idea for a romance novel, I'll write it."

The front door opened, and Bud strolled out, carting both Oliver and Sophie's suitcases. The kids trailed behind him with the grilled cheese sandwiches.

"Okay, say goodbye to your parents," Bud commanded

as he loaded the suitcases in one of the outdoor storage compartments.

Oliver hugged me first. "Do me a favor," I whispered in his ear. "Look out for Sophie. Trouble follows her."

He grinned. "I'll watch out for her."

"Good boy," I said, giving him one last squeeze.

Aidan scooped Sophie up and turned her upside down. "Promise you won't order pepperoni pizza without me," Sophie said in between bouts of laughter.

"Promise," I lied.

We stood on the porch steps and waved to them as they drove away.

I sighed and leaned my head against his shoulder. "Are you thinking what I'm thinking?" I asked.

"We just had grilled cheese."

"Appetizer," I stated. "I could easily crush a medium-sized Pepperoni pizza with extra cheese."

"You're trying to make me fat," he quipped.

"Yup. If you're fat, you can't run fast enough to get away from me."

"There's never any danger of that happening." He kissed the top of my head. "Besides, you're not one for running."

I grinned up at him. "You know me so well."

Chapter 2

"Taste this," Annie commanded.

"Hold on," I said. "I'm trying to placate my agent with evasive, golden-tongued fibs."

Annie sighed, but patiently waited for me to finish typing my email. I hit send and then clam-shelled my laptop.

"Okay, you have my undivided attention," I said to her.

She held out a wooden spoon toward me.

"What am I trying?" I asked.

"Plum butter," she said. "Careful, it's hot."

I hopped off the stool and went to her, grasping the wooden spoon. I dunked it into the huge pot simmering on the stove and then blew on the contents before gingerly sticking it in my mouth.

"Holy Moses," I muttered.

"I know, right?" She grinned. "I knew you'd love it."

"What are you going to do with it?"

"Well, now that I've perfected the recipe, I'm going to sell it at the Farmer's Market this weekend. You want to help me? The boys will be doing the beer thing, and I could use a helping hand."

"I'll help," I agreed. "On one condition."

She raised her brows and waited.

"You feed me while the boys are gone."

Annie laughed. "Let me guess, you want to crash here too?"

"Pretty please?"

She snorted. "The guest room is always ready and waiting. Matilda loves Jasper."

"He'll want to sleep on her bed. You cool with that?"

"Yeah, why not? We're about to cave and get her a puppy, but we're hoping we can last until Christmas."

I took a sip of water. "Good luck with that. Speaking of food, what are we having for dinner tonight?"

"Homemade butternut squash ravioli in a brown butter sauce. I just need to make a salad."

"Thank God you and Caleb moved Upstate. I'd starve without you."

"Every restaurant within a ten-mile radius knows your name and your usual order. Sometimes, the delivery guys just show up on your porch. That's serious power."

A few years ago, Annie had sold Mother Shucker and then she and Caleb had moved near us. It had taken her a little while to figure out her next move, but she'd really gotten into the farm-to-table-home-garden-canning-pioneer thing. I couldn't complain because I reaped the rewards of her cuisine and creativity.

Caleb and Aidan had started a brewing venture that included craft beer and meads. They were discussing adding ciders as well.

"Will you make the salad?" she asked.

"Sure thing."

"So, truth time," Annie said.

"Hmm?"

"Do you miss the twins?"

"Last night we ate pizza in front of the TV and went to bed at 8:30. This morning, Aidan and I both slept in and then we had morning boinkage. It was glorious."

"You didn't answer the question."

"Yeah, I miss them," I admitted. "But they're going to have a great time visiting the parks with the grandparents, and Aidan and I get to have some uninterrupted time together when he and Caleb get back from the brew festival."

Annie chuckled. "Oh, I miss the days of sleeping in. Matilda is better than any alarm clock."

I went to the refrigerator and pulled out all the ingredients for the salad. Annie had already grabbed me a cutting board, knife, and bowl.

"You know how a knife works, yes?" she teased. "Pointy end is sharp."

"Thanks for the reminder. Oliver's showing interest in cooking. If I send him to you for apprenticeship, will you take him? I need someone to cook for me in my old age. It's clear Sophie has my genes. She has no patience in the kitchen. Not to mention her destructive powers."

"How many appliances has she broken?"

"So far? Three. Sorry, four. She took out the blender the other day. We were making smoothies. She pushed a button, and sparks flew."

While I made the salad, Annie jarred the plum butter. We were finishing up when the front door opened and Caleb and Aidan strode into the kitchen, wearing matching baseball T-shirts and backwards caps.

"Why is that so hot?" Annie asked me.

"No idea, but it so is."

"Hello, women folk," Caleb said.

"Hello, men folk," I quipped. "Did you guys win?"

"Of course we won," Aidan said. "Gary pitched in the minors."

"Yeehaw," I said, tilting my head back so Aidan could kiss me on the lips.

"And thank you even more for not insisting we had to cheer you on from the stands," Annie said.

"And by cheer, she means heckle," I commented.

"But you're such good hecklers," Caleb said, moving to hug his wife. "Is Matilda up from her nap yet?"

"No. She went down late," Annie commented. "I'm letting her sleep."

Caleb walked over to the fridge and said, "What are we drinking?"

"Is any of the mead ready? I want to try it," I said.

"Yeah, I got a bottle in here." Caleb pulled out a bottle and poured it into three glasses.

"That's perfect," I said after taking a sip.

"You think?" Caleb asked. "I'm not sure."

Annie was in the middle of filling a pot of water when a door upstairs opened.

"The slumbering dragon is emerging," Annie quipped.

"I'll grab her," Caleb said, putting down his glass and heading for the stairs. "And see if I can fend off a post nap melt down."

"Are they not getting any better?" I asked Annie.

"Not really. She's just a monster until I get some food in her and then she's an angel."

Aidan and I set the table and grabbed a few bottles of salad dressing and stuck them on the table, along with the salad bowl.

Caleb returned with three-year-old Matilda who was squirming and growling.

"Better stick some food into that kid's mouth or she's gonna start howling," I commented.

"Not helpful," Annie said. She went to the freezer and pulled out a bag of chicken nuggets.

"I never thought I'd see the day where you had a kid that didn't like your gourmet cooking," I quipped.

"She has time to refine her palate," Annie said. She dumped a handful of chicken nuggets into the air fryer and quickly pressed a button.

My phone vibrated in my pocket. I pulled it out and looked at the screen.

"The kids?" Aidan asked.

I shook my head. "My mother." I silenced the call and let it roll to voicemail.

A few moments later, my phone beeped.

"She left a message," I said. "I'll call her back after dinner."

My phone stopped vibrating for a moment, and then immediately started up again.

"Might as well answer it," Aidan remarked. "She won't stop."

"Probably right," I agreed. I put the phone to my ear and walked out of the kitchen and into the living room. "Hello?"

"Sibby," Mom blubbered.

"What's wrong?" I asked immediately. "Is it Dad? *Bubbe*?"

"No. It's Aunt Ida. She passed away."

"Oh, that's terrible… Wait, who's Aunt Ida?"

"Aunt Ida. You know Aunt Ida. She's your second cousin twice removed."

I frowned in confusion. "If she's my second cousin twice removed, why are you calling her Aunt Ida?"

"Because she's older than your father, but younger than *Bubbe*," she said as if that explained everything.

"Oh, sure."

"She lived in Gator Springs, Florida. You remember Gator Springs, don't you?"

"Can't say that I do."

"Of course you remember," she protested. "Tiny little town off the Gulf coast in Florida. Ida had a big old house. We went for a visit once. Come on, you must remember."

"I really don't," I said. "Are you going to the funeral?"

"Ida didn't want a funeral. She's being cremated."

"Oh. Did she want—I mean did she leave instructions on how to handle her…everything?"

Mom was silent.

"Mom?" I prodded.

"She named you her legal heir."

"What?"

"She left everything to you, along with instructions on how to handle her remains."

"But why? I don't even remember this woman. How could she leave me everything?"

"Ida was quirky. And the black sheep of the family. You have that in common with her, you know. That's probably why she left everything to you."

"I'm not a black sheep…"

"I meant the quirky part."

"So, a woman I've never met, who I'm barely related to, has claimed me as her heir, or whatever?"

"You've met her before, you know," she insisted. "We went to visit her. I can't believe you don't remember."

"Well, I don't."

"This is really sad."

Sad? This woman was basically a stranger. I wasn't going to say that to my overly sensitive mother, though. My mom cried when she killed a spider.

"Were you close to her?"

"No. I barely knew her."

I closed my eyes and prayed for patience.

"Keep your phone on you. The lawyer will call you tomorrow."

"Okay," I said, rubbing the back of my neck. "I need to go. We're at Annie and Caleb's for dinner."

"Give them my love."

"Will do."

"And squeeze Matilda for me."

"I will," I said. "Bye, Mom."

I hung up with her and then headed back into the kitchen. Matilda was sitting at the table, chowing down on chicken nuggets.

"Dinner's just about ready," Annie said.

"Awesome," I said, setting my cell phone down on the table.

"How's Mom?" Aidan asked.

I sighed. "My family is nuts."

"You've inherited her residence in Gator Springs, along with her pink 1954 Cadillac convertible. Everything she left you was placed in a trust, so there's no waiting period like with a normal will. The deed and title have already been transferred to you," Luke Merrill said over the phone.

"The property taxes have also been paid for by the estate, so it's all up to date," he continued. "There was only one request."

"What's the request?"

"If you decide to sell the house, she wanted you to wait three months before moving forward with a sale."

I wasn't sure what to say.

"Have you been to Gator Springs?" he asked.

"Apparently. But I don't remember it."

"You should come down for a visit. Get a feel for the town."

"I'll think about it," I said.

"Excellent. Please give me a call if you have any questions, or if I can do anything else for you."

I hung up with Aunt Ida's lawyer and then leaned back in my office chair. Jasper jumped down from the bay window seat and launched himself into my lap.

"Missing the kids?" I asked him, scratching behind his ears which only made him push himself into me.

The French doors of my office were open, and Aidan appeared. "Hey," he said.

"Hey."

"So? What did the lawyer have to say?"

"I've inherited a house and a pink Cadillac convertible."

He whistled. "Sweet."

"I think I'm going to go down there and check it out," I said.

"Yeah?"

I nodded. "You're leaving for the beer festival in two days, and then it'll just be me and Jasper. I kind of want to see this house, figure out if we should sell it. My schedule is pretty open at the moment. It's like summer break from school, but like, the adult version."

Aidan scratched his jaw. "I could meet you down there, after the festival. Kind of like a mini vacation."

"That would be amazing," I said with a grin. "I need a good bronzing. My skin is Victorian vampire right now." I pointed my finger at him. "Don't say it."

"Say what?" He blinked owlishly. "I wasn't going to say anything."

"Not even about my inability to tan?"

"You said it, not me," he pointed out.

"Truth. I was thinking I could fly down there and just drive Aunt Ida's pink Cadillac. Oh, but Jasper."

I looked at the dog who had jumped off my lap and was currently rolling onto his back, legs spread, tongue hanging out of his mouth as he scratched his back along the rug.

"What are we going to do with Jasper?" I asked.

"My sister can watch him. She won't mind," he said.

"Oh good. He'll have fun terrorizing chickens. He deserves a mini vacation too."

"You okay?" Aidan asked.

"Hmm? Yeah, I'm okay. I'm just…I still don't get why she gave it all to me. I don't even know this woman. Though, Mom did say I've met her."

I stood up and went to Aidan, burying my face in his shirt. He smelled like clean laundry and sunshine.

"It doesn't feel right," I muttered.

"The woman didn't have any children," he pointed out. "And she clearly knew enough about you that she wanted you to inherit her home and car."

"Yeah, I guess."

He kissed the top of my head and stepped back. "Why don't we take Jasper for a walk? Get some fresh air. Hold hands without Sophie and Oliver chanting *ga-ross* in the background."

I grinned. "They really are my children."

Chapter 3

THE MIDDLE-AGED WOMAN on the plane sitting next to me couldn't stop staring at me.

Not that I blamed her.

My frizzy hair had its own zip code, and I was pretty sure my skin was in danger of melting off my face like that evil guy in *Raiders of the Lost Ark*.

She sat with her purse on her lap and every now and again she'd sigh.

On sigh number three, I looked at her. "May I help you with something?"

Her cheeks flushed in embarrassment. "Sorry, dear. I just, hold on a quick minute."

She opened her purse, riffled around in it for a moment, and then pulled out a comb.

"This might help," she said, offering it to me.

"Thanks," I said. "But it's a flaw in my genetics. The moment my hair knows we're going somewhere humid, it does this. And it's only gotten worse since I've had kids."

"Oh! You have kids?"

"Seven-year-old twins," I said. "Fraternal. A boy and a girl."

"I'd love to see pictures."

I pulled out my cell phone and then regaled a stranger on a plane for an hour with a slideshow of my children.

"Your daughter has quite the imagination," she commented, looking at a photo of Sophie in her Robin Hood costume but also wearing fairy wings.

"She's a trip," I said. "But I'm convinced my son is actually smart enough to do our taxes."

"Is that a polka dotted bow tie?"

"Yup."

"Precious."

"I know, right?"

I scrolled to the next photo and smiled down at the screen. It was a picture of the twins and Aidan on a Jon Boat. Sophie's grin was cheesy and toothy as she held up the fish she'd caught. Oliver looked squeamish and his nose was wrinkled, but he dutifully held the net.

"That's your husband?" she asked, her mouth dropping open.

"Yup."

"Oh my."

"Tell me about it," I said with a wry grin.

Once she got herself under control she asked, "What is it you do?"

"I'm an author."

"Oh! Fiction? Non-fiction?"

"Fiction."

"Like mystery and crime thrillers?"

Oh, boy.

"Like romance," I pitched my voice lower, "the dirty kind."

Her eyes widened and then she looked around as if she

was afraid that other people could hear our conversation. "I read a romance novel once. My husband very much liked the results of that."

My lips twitched, but I held back a smile. "I bet he did."

I also wrote children's books under a super-secret pen name that no one knew about except a few select people.

We spent the rest of the flight chatting about kids, and family, and why the both of us were going to Florida. I lied and told her I was going to Florida for a recharge. The lie was simpler than the truth: that I'd inherited a beach house from a woman I didn't even know.

The plane landed and we taxied to the gate. When we stopped, my companion unlatched her seatbelt and said, "It was nice chatting with you."

"You too."

"Enjoy Florida."

"I will, thank you."

She was halfway down the aisle before I was even up out of my seat. I reached for my suitcase in the overhead compartment, but I was too short to grab it. A college-aged kid helped me and said, "Here you go, ma'am."

Ma'am? Oy.

"Thank you," I said, hastily grabbing my shoulder bag and wheely suitcase and heading for the exit.

I went in the direction of baggage claim. As I stepped off the escalator, I looked around for a man who looked like he could be a lawyer. I expected someone in a suit with slicked back hair.

I did not expect a guy not much older than me in a pair of khakis, a salmon-colored polo, and brown boat shoes to be holding up a sign with my name on it.

"Mr. Merrill?" I asked as I approached.

"Please, call me Luke," he said with a wide smile. He held out his hand for me to shake.

"Luke," I repeated. "I'm Sibby. Nice to officially meet you. Thank you so much for offering to pick me up."

"My pleasure," he said. "Can I take your bag for you?"

"Oh, uh, sure. Thanks."

He was kind of dreamy in that *All American-surf's up* kind of way. It was unexpected. He'd sounded old on the phone. Not like a senior citizen, but I'd assumed he was my dad's age.

Nope.

"How was the flight?" he asked as he wheeled my suitcase toward the sliding doors.

"Fine. No turbulence."

"Always a plus."

The moment we stepped outside, a blast of hot, humid air hit me in the face. A startled gasp escaped my lips and I coughed.

"How are you not immediately sweating profusely," I wheezed. "I should've changed in the bathroom."

"Born and raised Floridian," he said. "I'm immune to the humidity." He looked at my hair and a grin spilled across his face. He unclipped the sunglasses from his shirt collar.

"I'm clearly not immune to the humidity," I remarked.

"I was trying to be polite and not mention the obvious."

"When my hair realizes we're going to a tropical climate, it instantly rebels. No idea why."

Luke grinned and slid the sunglasses onto his nose. "We're at the end of this row."

The silver Beamer was sleek and luxurious, and more importantly, it had a powerful air conditioning vent. I stuck my face in front of it without any shame.

"So, I only briefly looked at a map. Gator Springs is about forty-five minutes from the airport, right?" I asked.

"Yeah. Are you hungry? Do you want me to hit a drive thru on our way back?"

"No, I'm okay. Thanks."

I pulled my phone out of my shoulder bag and sent off a text to Aidan and another to Annie, letting them know I was en route to my destination.

"So, you're a Floridian. Were you born and raised in Gator Springs?" I asked.

"No. I'm from Tampa. I practiced law for a few years up in New York and hated it so much that I came back to Florida and opened my own practice. Sorry, am I being too chatty?"

"Nope, you're good. Even though I haven't lived in the city for years, I still instinctively balk when someone is friendly. Give me a few minutes, I'll get used to it." My messy bun was sliding to the side, and I quickly redid it, hoping to keep the frizz out of my face. "Gator Springs must be a pretty special place if it made you open up a shop of your own."

"Pretty special," he agreed.

"Tell me about it. I don't know anything."

"I think I'll let you discover its charm for yourself." He drove us out of the airport parking lot, and we quickly made our way to the interstate.

"So, your mother is an interesting woman," Luke said.

"Oh, you spoke to her?"

"Yeah. Ida had a number listed for your mother, but not for you. So, I called her to get your information. She had a lot to say.

"Whatever she said, I take no responsibility for it," I warned.

He chuckled. "Nothing bad, I swear. She had a lot of

lovely things to say about you. That's all. She said you're a writer?"

"Yep." I didn't elaborate.

"And your husband owns a small brewery with his best friend?"

"Wow, how long were you guys on the phone?"

"Fifteen minutes."

"And you learned all that?"

"She's also really proud of the twins and their roles in last year's Thanksgiving play."

"Sophie was head turkey," I said, feeling myself puff up with pride. "Her brother played the butcher and carved her for dinner."

"Sounds gruesome."

"It was."

He chuckled.

"You married?" I asked.

"Nope. Not a lot of women in my dating age bracket in Gator Springs. I've had a few offers to become arm candy, but I want more for myself."

"So, the average age demographic of Gator Springs is…"

"Seventy-two. It's a sleepy little town where everyone knows everyone. There's one salon, one bar, and a small General Store that has everything from groceries, to clothing, to souvenirs. Anything truly specific and you have to drive to a city."

"You don't get bored?" I asked. "Living in such a small town?"

"Your mother also said you live in a small town in Upstate New York?"

"Touché. Though to be fair, I have a husband, a dog, and two children who keep me wildly entertained."

"I walk my dog every morning on the beach, and he

comes with me to work. He wanted to come with me to the airport, but the Beamer is a two-seater, as you've noticed. I moved to Gator Springs and threw out all my suits. I wear khakis, polos, and boat shoes. I fish on the weekends. I play golf. I have fun."

"Don't take this the wrong way, but *you* kind of sound seventy-two."

"I don't go to bed before ten."

"Phew, I was worried for a minute."

"You're such a New Yorker," he said with a laugh. "Five minutes in my car and you're already busting my chops."

"Sorry."

"Don't worry about it. I enjoy the conversation. Usually, I have to hear about gallstones and colonoscopies. This is refreshing."

I looked out the window, marveling at all the palm trees. "You don't get sick of sunshine?"

"Nope."

"What about hurricanes?"

"They're not that bad. I think we've had one storm that destroyed some homes, but that was fifty years ago. Look, it sounds like you're hunting for reasons to dump this house, but I'm going to try to convince you to go in with an open mind."

"I never said I was going to dump this house."

"You're thinking about it, aren't you?"

"I'm not *not* thinking about it."

He changed lanes and then said, "Give it a chance. Besides, you just inherited a house in a beach town. Think about the yearly vacations. How bad could that be?"

"Wow, you really are a lawyer."

Chapter 4

As we approached Gator Springs, there was an old wooden sign painted green and gold with a carving of an alligator on it, and a strange white stripe down the alligator's back.

Welcome to Gator Springs, Florida. Population 342.

"You're kidding," I said. "Three hundred and forty-two people live in Gator Springs?"

"Actually, it's three hundred and forty, now. Aunt Ida passed away, and so did Burt."

"Burt? Who's Burt?"

"The mascot of Gator Springs. He's like the OG."

"Mascot? You mean—are you seriously talking about the alligator on the sign?"

"Yep. He had a long life. He was over fifty years old. Some think he was closer to sixty, but it's not like we could ask him."

"You can't count an alligator as part of the population of a town."

"Yes, we can."

I was starting to understand why eccentric Aunt Ida had settled in quirky Gator Springs.

We'd turned off the highway and after the sign for the town, the foliage had grown thicker, the trees bent and blocked out most of the sky and sun.

"You have to be careful driving into town," Luke explained. "Deer like to pop out of the brush at twilight. So many drivers have swerved, trying not to hit them, and wound up in the bog. There's no cell service in the bog, so unless someone drives by and sees your car, you're stuck."

"Bogs? Alligators? Only one bar in town? You're really selling this place," I commented.

"Beach."

"Right. There is that."

"This is Main Street," Luke said. "The town finally put in a streetlight, but this used to be a four-way stop."

I looked out the window at the shops and buildings. They were quaint but freshly painted. I'd expected a chic beach motif, but there was nothing kitschy about it.

"There's Bob's," Luke pointed out. "The only bar in town. But they serve food and it's pretty good. Nothing like New York, though."

"There's no place I've ever been that serves food like New York."

"My office," Luke said, gesturing to a whitewashed wood building that resembled a beach cottage. "Aunt Ida's residence is only a few blocks out of town."

"Why do you call her Aunt Ida?"

"She was everyone's Aunt Ida here," he explained. "She was a big part of this town. Everyone adored her. We're sorry she's gone."

"My mom didn't tell me how she passed," I said suddenly. "I just got a call that she *had* passed."

"In her sleep."

"Well, if you've got to go, that's the way to do it," I said softly.

We drove down a long, windy road and at the end of it stood a three-story house with balconies on both the second and third floors. A large wooden porch swing with bright red pillows beckoned to be sat in.

There was a detached one car garage which I knew had the pink Cadillac inside.

"She lived here all alone?" I asked. "This place is *huge*."

"It was always filled with people," Luke said. "And stray animals." He parked the Beamer along the curb and then hopped out to grab my suitcase.

I took my shoulder bag and headed up to the porch. "Ah, I don't have keys."

"I have a set for you," he said, wheeling my suitcase to the front steps. "But in case you lose them, there's a spare set underneath the alligator statue." He pointed to a small stone alligator that was nestled among the bushes at the front of the house.

He removed a set of keys from his keyring and placed them in my palm. "You have my number. If you need anything, please let me know."

"Thanks again for picking me up from the airport," I said.

"Sure thing."

I waited until he got back into his Beamer and started the engine before waving. He waved back and then drove off, leaving me alone. It was mid-afternoon and between the heat, humidity, and the travel, I was ready for a nap and a cocktail. Or maybe just a cocktail.

I found the key to the lock of the front door and slid it in. With a sigh, I turned the knob and pushed the door open. The front hallway was dark, and I fumbled around, attempting to find a light switch.

There was a porcelain light cover near the door, and I flipped the switch.

"Oh. My. God." My eyes widened as I took in the decor.

My phone rang and I riffled through my shoulder bag, my mouth still hanging open in shock.

"Hello?" I greeted.

"Hey, have you arrived yet?" Annie asked.

"Uh, yeah. I'm actually standing in the foyer."

"And?"

"Aunt Ida lived in a den of iniquity, fit for a vampire."

"Say what now?"

"Everything is like, red velvet and fake candle lighting," I commented. I stepped deeper into the house. There was a pair of French doors which were currently closed. I opened them and groaned.

"What?" Annie demanded. "What is it?"

"I found the salon. Vintage brass lamps with pink lampshades and tassels."

"So, less vampire den of iniquity and more nineteenth-century brothel?"

"Yeah, it's looking that way. There's a fireplace. That's cool."

"How's the air?"

"What do you mean?"

"I mean, it's Florida. Tell me there's air-conditioning."

"There's air-conditioning. Actually, it's like an ice box in here. So at least that's good."

I pulled back the red velvet drapes on the front window to let in natural light. The sofa and couch were covered in a big pink rose pattern. It bordered on garish.

I went to the fireplace mantle and counted three black boxes with name placards on the front of them. "Tilly, Artemis, Bilbo…"

"What are those names of?"

"No idea," I muttered. There was a picture of an older woman with gray hair, wearing an orange and yellow muumuu, cuddling three cats.

"Ah, I think I have an idea," I said. "She had her cats cremated—and they're resting on the mantle for all eternity."

"You're kidding."

"Oh, I wish I was. I'm scared to go upstairs now."

"Go upstairs," she urged. "I want to know how it looks."

I left my shoulder bag and luggage in the foyer and gingerly headed up the front stairs. "Okay, there are four doors and they're all closed. You know what this place reminds me of?"

"What?"

"Those old school boarding houses from the fifties." I opened the first door and immediately closed it. "Yikes."

"What?" Annie demanded.

"Aunt Ida had a thing for china dolls."

"Say no more."

I opened the second door and let out a sigh of relief. "Just a bathroom."

"Good. That's good. Next?"

I traipsed to the end of the hallway and opened the door. "This looks like a guest bedroom. Brass bed with an old quilt and an antique wash basin."

"The house sounds like a real hodge-podge."

"It's got character, that's for sure."

The last bedroom on the landing was the master. The bed was a huge, heavy, canopy bed with thick blue drapes that were currently tied back.

"Oh, this bathroom is unreal," I said when I opened another door.

"Picture?"

"Hang on." I fiddled with my phone and took a photo of the bathroom, complete with a clawfoot porcelain tub.

"That's gorgeous," Annie said. "Original?"

"I think so. What a strange house. There's a third floor."

"I'll stay on the phone. I want a play by play."

I took the second flight of stairs up to the third floor which turned out to be the attic and it was filled with boxes, trunks, and old paintings in ornate frames.

"There's a lot of stuff up here," I said, reaching for a box out of sheer curiosity. I opened it and found stacks of photos. I closed it up again.

"What kind of stuff?" Annie asked.

"The kind of stuff people want to save but only so they can look at it once every ten years."

"I've got boxes like that. From my parents' house. I still haven't gone through them. Out of sight out of mind."

"Sounds about right."

I left the attic and headed back downstairs. "I'm now going into the kitchen." It was outdated but clean. The floor was covered in a blue flower linoleum and the counters were made of some sort of yellow laminate from the seventies.

"Well? How's the kitchen?" Annie demanded.

"It would offend your chef's sensibilities." I went to the refrigerator that hummed loudly. There was nothing in it aside from a box of baking soda. In the freezer, there was a bottle of vodka.

"Either Aunt Ida never cooked, or someone cleaned out her fridge," I said, removing the bottle of vodka. "The woman left behind a bottle of Smirnoff. Sorry, Smirnoff Raspberry."

"Yuck."

"Beggars can't be choosers." I unscrewed the bottle and took a sip. "Well, aside from the creepy china doll room, I haven't seen anything too—no way."

"No way what? What?" Annie demanded.

"Hang on." I took the bottle of vodka, and with the phone to my ear, I went to the back door. I opened it and let out a loud whoop.

"You're not going to fucking believe this," I stated. "I'm like five hundred feet from the ocean."

"You're not."

"I am!" I took another swig of vodka. "This. Is. Paradise."

Chapter 5

OKAY, this kind of doesn't suck.

I plopped down onto the beach. I set the bottle of vodka aside and removed my shoes. As I sunk my toes into the cool sand, I called Aidan. "Guess where I am right now."

"You're in Gator Springs," Aidan commented.

"Yes."

"So, I guessed correctly."

I laughed. "Get more specific than Gator Springs."

"Aunt Ida's house."

"The beach *behind* Aunt Ida's house."

"What?"

"Yup. Nice little discovery, if I do say so myself."

"Did you remember to pack a bathing suit?"

"Did I remember...wait a second." I smacked my forehead. "I forgot to pack a bathing suit."

"Who goes to Florida and forgets a bathing suit?"

"Um, the same kind of person who forgets to pack the SPF 75. Oliver is going to lecture me if he finds out."

He chuckled. "We won't tell him. So, how's the house?"

"It's not too bad, actually. It feels kind of weird, though. To be enjoying the beach and the house knowing how we got it."

"It's not like you befriended an old woman and tricked her into putting you into her will."

"True. I can't believe people actually do that. Sinister. Would make a good plot for a book, though." I shook my head. "How's the festival?"

"It's a bunch of smelly, unwashed men with neck beards all vying for the blue ribbon of best brew."

"You're loving every second of it, aren't you?" I asked with a laugh.

"I am," he agreed. "Miss you though. And the kids."

"Well, you'll be down here before you know it. I better get going. I want to check out the town before the sun sets. I'll go on foot so I can get the lay of the land."

"Don't do anything I wouldn't do."

"Like karaoke?"

"And break dancing."

"Duly noted."

"I love you," he said. "Text me when you get home. I want to know you're safe."

"I guess I forgot to mention the average age of the occupants of Gator Springs is seventy-two years old."

"Hey, old people get new hips and then they're like, ready to rumble."

"How much beer have you had?"

"A good amount. The last one was a Belgian tripel."

"Say hi to Caleb," I said. "Talk later?"

"Sounds good. Love you."

"Love you, too."

I hung up with Aidan, feeling all squishy and warm

inside. I wasn't sure if that was due to the love I felt for my husband or the vodka. Maybe a bit of both.

I could've stayed on the beach longer, and I promised myself that the following night I'd watch the sun set.

But there was nothing in the refrigerator, and I didn't want to wake up without coffee.

There were some things in life I could forgo. Caffeine in the morning was not one of them.

I wandered back to the house and up the stairs to the master bedroom. I opened my suitcase and pulled out my bright pink fanny pack and grabbed my wallet from my shoulder bag. I locked up the house and set out in the direction of town. Before I'd gone to sit on the beach, I'd changed into a pink tank top, a pair of clam diggers, and an old pair of white Keds. My hair was curling against my temples and neck, despite it being up in a messy bun.

Though the sun was aloft and bright, there were several big trees that blotted out the sky on my way into town. The cool breeze from the ocean cut the sweltering heat.

I was about to pass Bob's when my stomach began rumbling and I thought it was a good idea to eat something instead of shopping on an empty stomach.

I opened the front door and stepped inside. There were three old men wearing Hawaiian shirts and flip flops sitting at the bar with pints of beer in front of them.

"Can I help you?" the aging bartender asked as he wiped down the bar and then threw the rag over his curved shoulder.

"I heard you served food here."

"We do," the bartender said. He reached for a laminated menu and chucked it down at the spot in the corner.

I took a step forward, my foot sinking into the floor. I looked down.

Sand.

I finally noted the decor. Pink flamingo lights were strung up along the wood paneled walls. The ceiling had fishing nets tacked to it and far too many dried sea horses, starfish and iron anchors.

"My name is Norm," the bartender said, rubbing his salt-and-pepper beard.

"Nice to meet you, I'm Sibby."

"Sibby," the guy in the blue Hawaiian shirt commented. "That's an interesting name."

"Sibby," another man said. "That name sounds familiar."

"I've inherited Aunt Ida's house," I explained.

"Oh, so you're the one," Norm said. "Sit. Have a look at the menu."

I took the seat where Norm pointed, trying to ignore the curious stares of the three occupants of the bar—four —including Norm. I picked up the menu and flipped it over. A giant raccoon's face peered up at me, along with what looked like a story of the bar's conception.

I quickly skimmed the back of the menu. "Wait, is this —is the bar named after a raccoon?"

"Yup," Norm said.

"Bob. Bob the Raccoon? I just want to make sure I have this correct."

"You have it correct," one of the guys said. "I'm Oscar."

"I'm Bill," his friend in the blue Hawaiian print shirt added.

"And I'm Ralph," the third man said.

"Nice to meet you," I said.

"So, what'll you have?" Norm asked.

"Oh, uh, how about the house special," I said.

"You sure you don't want to look at the menu?" Norm asked.

"I'm adventurous. And a glass of water, please."

"You got it." Norm filled up a glass of water and set it down in front of me, and then he disappeared behind a swinging door into what I assumed was the kitchen.

Snap, Crackle, and Pop all stared at me, and I shot them an awkward smile.

"So, you're from New York?" Ralph asked.

"Yeah, I'm from New York." I ran a finger along the edge of the bar. "Does everyone in this town know each other's business?"

"Yup," Bill said. "Small town, not a lot happens here. What are you going to do with Aunt Ida's place?"

"You know it was built in the 1900s, right?" Oscar said before I could reply. "It's actually a historical building. You're not allowed to change the structure of it, so if you were thinking of remodeling, you have to talk to the Historic Preservation Society and get the right permits."

I blinked. "I just rolled into town a few hours ago. I haven't decided what I'm going to do with the house."

The swinging door to the kitchen opened and Norm returned, carrying a bowl of soup. He set it down in front of me and then handed me a spoon. "I'll wait."

"Wait for what?" I asked.

"For you to taste it."

"What is it?" I leaned over the bowl and gave it a sniff. "Smells good."

"Of course it smells good. It's my Maw Maw's recipe, with a secret ingredient so special I haven't even told my wife what it is."

I scooped up a bite, paused for a few moments to make sure it was cool, and then stuck the spoon in my mouth. "Oh my God, this is *incredible*."

Norm grinned and the three guys at the bar chuckled.

I all but inhaled the bowl of stew, wondering if I had it in me for another serving.

"Okay, I'm curious. What did I just eat?" I asked, pushing the empty bowl away.

Norm took the bowl and said, "Gator stew."

The General Mercantile store was closed. Small town hours, apparently. They'd open back up the next morning at seven. Norm and the others hadn't thought to tell me that.

I wandered back to the house, my belly pleasantly full of gator stew. The bit of vodka I drank had long since disappeared from my system.

There was no TV in the salon, nor in any of the bedrooms. I could've read or watched something on my phone, but I went up to the attic instead.

I stared around at all the boxes, feeling trapped by them. They weren't mine. Well, legally, they were, but it felt like I was invading Ida's privacy. These were her belongings that she'd loved enough to want to keep. But it seemed like a shame to keep things boxed away and out of sight.

With a sigh, I dove in. I was bored and curious, and they'd have to be gone through at some point.

I found a box full of old clothes and costume jewelry. Smiling, I set them aside for Sophie, knowing we'd have fun playing dress-up.

My phone rang, but I couldn't find it. It was buried underneath mounds of faux velvet.

I finally found it and answered. "Hello, heathens."

Sophie's face appeared through the screen, covered in barbecue sauce. She gave me a toothy grin. Oliver was in the process of wiping his hands with a wet nap. He was wearing a red bowtie. Only my son would wear a bowtie to eat barbecue.

"Hi, Mom," Oliver said.

"Are you having fun with Grandma and Grandpa?" I asked.

"Grandma says I have to take off my Robin Hood costume so she can wash it," Sophie complained. "But it's not that dirty. Promise."

"Listen to Grandma. She knows everything."

"Do you miss us?" Oliver asked.

"More than you know. But I'll be seeing you before you know it. What did you have for dinner?"

"I had baby back ribs, fried okra, hush puppies, and I'm about to eat a key lime pie," Sophie announced.

"And you, Ollie?"

"Brisket, corn bread, and mashed potatoes."

Even though I was full, that all sounded delicious. "Aren't you going to ask me what I had for dinner?"

"What did you have for dinner?" Sophie asked, licking her finger clean of sauce.

"Gator stew."

"Gross." She wrinkled her nose.

"It was good," I insisted. "Look what I found..." I

pulled out a floppy red hat and a pink boa and put them on.

"So pretty!" Sophie said.

"Where are you?" Ollie asked.

"I'm in Aunt Ida's attic, going through some boxes."

A few days ago, when I'd told the twins I was going to Florida, I'd tried to explain how Ida was related to us. It had been confusing, so I'd settled for just calling her our great aunt.

"What else did you find?" Oliver asked, clearly intrigued.

"Nothing else yet. I just started going through stuff. But when I find something I think you'll like, I'll tell you."

"Oh, dessert is here," Sophie said. "Bye, Mom. Love you!"

"Love you too. Ollie, don't let her eat that entire piece of pie herself."

He smiled. "I won't. Bye, Mom. Love you a lot."

"Love you, kiddo."

I hung up with the kids and got back to it. I found an old coin collection which I knew Oliver would love, so I set it aside for him.

Only when my butt went numb did I finally quit. I stood up and stretched my arms over my head, pausing mid-yawn when I heard the stairs creak.

I listened for a moment and heard the creak again, only this time it sounded like the wood was moaning.

"Snap out of it," I said, shaking my head. "It's an old beach house. No need to let your imagination run wild."

The attic light flickered and then went out.

"Okay, seriously? I've heard of weird things happening in New Orleans, but this is Gator Springs. Is this about the hat and the boa? I'll put them back." I quickly removed them and set them down on the box.

The lights flickered back on.

"This is really creeping me out." I quickly left the attic and headed down to the second-floor master bedroom.

I went into the bathroom and looked at my reflection. My hair was the size of a small country, and my skin was pin prickled with goosebumps.

"Hot bath," I said, still talking out loud to myself because I felt less alone that way. It was either talk to myself or get a china doll and hang out with it, but that was also too creepy for words.

I sat on the edge of the tub and while the water ran, I called Annie.

"I think this house is haunted," I blurted out.

"You drank the rest of the Smirnoff, didn't you?"

"What? No! I'm not inebriated, I swear. I think this house might be haunted."

"Is this like the time we were in college you and told me a bat had flown in through the open window and was zooming around the living room and when I got there, there was no trace of a bat?"

"No, this isn't like that time. And for the record, there really was a bat."

"Okay, I'm bored. Matilda is asleep and I can't find anything good on Netflix. You pay for all these subscription services and there's nothing ever on."

"Annie?"

"Yeah? Oh, right, sorry. I'm focusing. So, the house is haunted? What makes you think so."

"If I tell you, you can't make fun of me. I'm all alone down here and sure, there might be a small chance that I'm overreacting, but—"

"I won't make fun of you," she promised. "What happened to make you think the house is haunted?"

"So I was in the attic, going through some boxes.

Found some really cool clothes and costume jewelry, by the way. Anyway, I put on the floppy hat and boa."

"Uh, okay. I don't see how—"

"I heard a stair creak."

"It's an old house."

"That's what I thought, but there's no one else here, and then the lights flickered off."

"Maybe there was wind. You know, it is Florida, so hurricanes and tropical storms—"

"I asked if I should take off the boa and hat just messing around, but when I actually took them off, the lights came back on."

Annie paused.

"Weird, right?"

"Kinda weird," Annie admitted. "Maybe a raccoon was gnawing on some wires or something."

"Maybe. I kinda wish I'd driven down and brought Jasper. I haven't been alone in a house by myself in years. This is just loneliness. Yep. That's all this is. Loneliness."

"You're not alone. You have china dolls and cat ashes on the mantle to keep you company."

"Yeah, not helping the wigging-out factor. I'm taking a bath and then going to bed."

"Keep me posted on the ghostly stuff. Let me know if you see any weird silvery apparitions."

"Are you trying to keep me awake for all eternity?"

"No. But I'm your best friend."

"You said you wouldn't make fun of me."

"I'm not making fun of you," she insisted. She fell silent.

"What? What is it?"

"Remember that kid we went to college with? What was his name. Jason Perk? He was from Charleston, and he did ghost tours. He swore he saw an Old Confederate soldier ghost one time when he was giving a tour of the jail."

"Seriously, Annie. You're not helping."

"Sorry. But he did say that the ghost wasn't malevolent. He just kinda followed him on his tour and whispered facts into his ear."

"Worst. Friend. Ever."

"Hey, you're the one that ditched me when you promised you'd help me at the Farmer's Market. And now you're having way more fun than I am."

"More fun? I'm all alone in a haunted house. How is that fun? And you said you were cool with me ditching you. Why are you acting prickly?"

"I'm not acting prickly. At least I didn't think I was. Sorry. I don't like it when Caleb's gone. The house feels very empty without him."

"That's called love."

"Maybe I'm just used to the sound of him snoring."

"Isn't that romantic," I drawled.

"That's called marriage."

Chapter 6

I WAS AWAKENED the next morning by a strong round of knocking on the front door. It had taken me a long time to fall asleep due to my irrational brain turning over the idea that the house was actually haunted. When I finally did get to sleep, I was spread diagonal across the bed, three pillows over my head.

Bleary-eyed and confused, I stumbled down the stairs, wondering who was at the house this early in the morning. As I approached the front door, the grandfather clock in the hallway told me it wasn't as early as I thought it was. It was just past eight.

I opened the front door, letting in a blast of heat and humidity. It was like getting a facial for free.

A woman wearing a blue halter dress with a sweetheart neckline, big blonde curls, and bright red lips stood on the porch steps.

"Good morning!" she chirped.

I blinked and then shielded my eyes from the sun. "Morning," I mumbled.

"I'm sorry. Did I wake you?"

"It's fine," I said.

She held up a casserole dish. "I came to welcome you to town. My name is Betty Sue Mason and I live on the other side of Main Street."

"Oh, thanks," I said, taking the casserole that Betty Sue was thrusting into my hands.

"If you need anything, don't be afraid to ask. We take care of our own." She pointed to the casserole. "Heat it in the oven at 425 for fifteen minutes. It'll give the top a nice little crunch."

"Thank you. That was sweet of you. What is it?" I asked, peering beneath the tin foil.

"Gator and scrambled egg frittata."

Of course it is.

"Oh…yum."

"My mother owns the only salon in town—Curl up and Dye. Anyway, you should stop by."

I instantly touched my hair, wishing I'd thought to look in a mirror before answering the door.

"Oh, I didn't mean there was anything wrong with your hair. I just meant, that's where all the ladies congregate for coffee and a chat."

"Thanks for the invite," I said. "I'll stop by."

She beamed. "Well, I'll get out of your hair. Ha! See what I did there? Anyway, hope to see you around town!"

"Thanks for the food, Betty Sue."

With a smile and a wave, I closed the door. I trudged into the kitchen with the casserole dish and immediately put it into the fridge.

Now that I was awake, I remembered there was no coffee in the house. No groceries, either.

I stumbled back upstairs and splashed water on my face and brushed my teeth. I threw on a pair of yoga pants, a purple T-shirt, and my tennis shoes.

Bob's was open and I took a chance that they served coffee.

"Yeah, we got coffee," Norm said. "None of that fancy pants Starbucks though. So, if you want a chai half calf skim caramel whipped thingy, we don't make it."

"That was oddly specific." I blinked. "Good thing I just want a plain old coffee. The biggest size you've got, and to-go please."

"I don't do to-go," Norm said.

"Seriously?" I asked.

He nodded. "You can take a mug if you want, but you have to promise to bring it back."

"I'll bring it back," I promised.

Norm reached underneath the bar and grabbed a mug. He poured coffee into it and then placed it in front of me.

"Any cream?" I asked hopefully.

"Nope."

I sighed and reached into my bag for my wallet. I pulled out a few bills and set them on the bar. "Thanks."

I picked up the cup which had *#1 Dad* flaking off it and left the bar. I slid my sunglasses down onto my nose and headed for the General Mercantile store. Thankfully, it was open. I snatched a carton of half and half, and there in the dairy section, poured it into my coffee.

Because I wasn't feeding children at the moment and therefore didn't have to set a good example, I got a mix of healthy stuff along with the necessary junk food staples. Hershey's Syrup, Twizzlers, and a carton of ice cream. It was only when I got up to the register that I realized that I'd gotten way too many groceries to carry home.

"Rats," I muttered.

"Sibby?"

I looked up from staring at my full cart to find Luke carrying a basket that was only filled with a few items.

Today, he was dressed in a pair of khakis, a lavender polo and brown boat shoes.

"Oh, hi."

"Good morning," he greeted with a smile. "Did you just say *rats*?"

"Uh, yeah. I have kids. It's my version of a curse word."

"You're cursing why?"

"I didn't drive," I said. "And I have a lot of groceries."

"I'll drive you home."

"You don't have to do that," I protested. "You're clearly here to do your own shopping."

"I don't mind."

"What about your practice?"

"What about it?"

"Don't you have to go to work?"

"Do you think lawyers just sit around in their office, waiting for clients to call?"

"Well, yeah."

"That's what cell phones are for."

I sighed. "You sure you don't mind?"

"I wouldn't have offered if I minded."

"Okay, well, thanks."

And because it was a small town where everyone knew everyone, I ended up making polite conversation with Dolores. She worked the register, but she and her husband owned the store.

Luke helped me load the groceries into his Beamer and I made sure I'd drunk enough of my coffee so that there was no chance of me spilling it in his car.

"It feels really dumb to have you drive me four blocks," I commented. "I could've gone home and grabbed the car and come back."

"But why? I was here already. I don't mind helping out

a neighbor. So, I heard you went to Bob's last night for dinner."

"Nothing is a secret around here, is it?" I asked.

Luke pulled up to the house and parked. "Not really. There's not that much to do around here, so people talk."

"You mean gossip?"

"Gossip implies nefarious intent."

"Ah." I got out of his car and then went to unlock the house before unloading the groceries. "I met Betty Sue this morning."

"Did you?"

"She brought over a gator and scrambled egg frittata."

"How was it?"

"It's still in the fridge."

Luke helped me with the groceries and set them on the counter in the kitchen.

"She was very welcoming," I commented.

"I bet she was," Luke said. "She's been after Aunt Ida's house for years. She wants to turn it into a bed and breakfast. Don't be surprised if she makes you an offer."

"So, the reptile and egg frittata is something like a bribe?"

"Or at least a way to butter you up. Did she butter you?"

"That sounded weird. And no. I don't think she buttered me."

"So, do you like the place?"

"I do," I said slowly, not wanting to mention my worry that the house was haunted. I pulled out a bag of coffee and filters. "So far, I don't really see a downside to the house. I mean, it's within walking distance of the beach. You conveniently forgot to mention that yesterday, or on the phone when you called to give me the news about Aunt Ida."

"But how much better was the discovery?" he asked.

"Yeah, okay. You want a cup of coffee?"

"Nah. I better get going. I promised I'd take Joey for a walk."

"Your dog?"

"Nope. Client. My dog's name is Scottie."

"Your—you know what? Never mind. I don't want to know. Thanks for your help, Luke."

"Any time. Don't see me out. I've got it."

A few minutes later, the smell of coffee wafted through the dated kitchen. I stood at the kitchen sink and looked out the window. The sun was shining, there wasn't a cloud in the sky, so I grabbed my cup of joe and walked to the beach.

<hr>

Chapter 7

<hr>

"JUST EXPLAIN IT TO ME," Alex said, her face peering at me through the computer screen.

"I've explained it to you a dozen times," I said to my agent. "I'm not done writing romance. But I'm not going to churn out crap just for the hell of it. When I have a story to write, I'll write it. And pressure from you isn't going to make me want to do it."

"We've worked together for several years," she said. "I'd like to think you can tell me the truth."

"You're relentless," I stated.

"But there's more, isn't there?" she demanded. "I know there is."

"Things were really crazy there for a bit," I reminded her. "What with the book adaption to the big screen. It was a dream come true, but it kind of did a number on me. My name in the media, the tags on social. It got to be too much."

I'd all but retreated from social media and had thrown myself into other projects. Different projects that had nothing to do with being Sibby Goldstein.

It sounded stupid, right? Like a lot of kids, I'd wanted to be famous. Fame and fortune and all that jazz. Well, it happened. A book of mine had been adapted to the big screen with the help of one of the most famous celebrities in Hollywood.

Jolie Kingston had believed in me and my stories. With her connections, a dream of mine had come true. She'd been cast in the lead female role, which showed off her acting chops. It had taken her from Hollywood rom-com girl to something more. She'd showed her depth and her ability to play versatile roles.

After the furor of the movie died down, I'd retreated. The house Upstate had been renovated completely, the twins were growing, and I'd pulled back from the world entirely. And then my writing had gone in a different direction.

I'd started writing children's books and had asked Nat to illustrate. It breathed a new avenue of creativity into me and had given me a purpose. It had also kept me out of the limelight because all of those books were published under a secret pen name.

Alex reached for her cup of coffee, no doubt it was her fourth of the day already. "Okay, I'll stop pressuring you."

"Really?"

"Probably not."

"Well, at least you're honest."

I got off the call and closed my computer. My stomach rumbled, reminding me that I hadn't yet eaten breakfast.

I heated up a slice of gator and egg frittata, closed my eyes, and took a bite. "Well, I stand corrected," I muttered.

It was freaking delicious. Even better after I added some hot sauce.

After I ate, I hopped in the shower and then decided to

check out the pink Cadillac. The garage was air conditioned, and it had kept the car in perfect shape. I whistled, gliding my hand over the tail fins. There wasn't even a scratch on the paint.

I slid into the front seat of the car and gripped the steering wheel for a moment. The black leather seats were well loved, but not cracked or broken. I opened the glove compartment, laughing when I found a pink polka dotted head scarf. I immediately tied it around my hair and then I slid the key into the ignition.

The vehicle had an old-school radio, and when the car started with a massive rumble, the Beach Boys filtered through the speakers, bringing a huge smile to my face.

I took in a deep breath and backed out of the garage. With my sunglasses perched on my nose and "Sloop John B" blaring, everything slipped away. I had no responsibilities, no one to feed except myself, and for the first time in a long time, I didn't have to think about anyone else. My time was mine, and it was glorious.

I drove slowly, the engine chugging along as I went down Main Street. The salon was at the end of the road on the corner. The sign for Curl Up and Dye looked like it hadn't been touched since the eighties. I parked the beast of a convertible on the opposite side of the street, thanking my lucky stars I didn't have to parallel park.

The salon felt very Steel Magnolias. Quaint shop, tons of photos on the walls, and plants on the windowsill. There were two women in the salon, both in their mid to late sixties.

"Be right with you, sugar," the woman with teased hair said. "Look down for me, Ellie."

Ellie bent her neck and stared at her lap.

I took a seat in the front waiting area and reached for a

magazine that had Jolie Kingston on the cover. I grinned as I skimmed the article that was talking about Jolie's new TV show. She was playing a college kid despite being in her early thirties.

"I just love Jolie Kingston," the woman in the chair said. "I read that article and she seems really down to earth."

"She is," I said before I could stop myself.

"You've met her?" the woman cutting hair asked.

Oops.

"Um, yeah, I've met Jolie."

"What's she like?" Ellie asked, peering at me from underneath wet bangs.

"Ellie, don't move, or you're going to wind up with an angular bob."

"Sorry," Ellie said. "I'm just really curious about Jolie."

"She's nice," I said.

"Nice? That's it? I need more," Ellie demanded.

Mayday, Mayday.

"Wait, you're Sibby, aren't you?" the hair stylist asked.

"Yes, that's me."

"You met my daughter this morning. I'm Jeannie."

"Nice to meet you. Betty Sue told me to stop by," I replied. I patted my frizzy ponytail. "I wasn't really—I mean, I don't need a haircut or anything, but she mentioned this was the place for a coffee and a chat."

"Gator Springs doesn't have a designated coffee shop, so this place kinda fills that void. Pour yourself a cup." She gestured to the coffee station that had a full pot of black coffee.

"I'm good for now, actually. Thanks."

"Sibby," Ellie repeated. "Why does that name sound familiar?"

"I inherited Aunt Ida's place," I explained. "I'm down here to get some things sorted."

"No, that's not how I know your name," Ellie murmured. She frowned in pensive thought and then she smiled. "You're the author."

"Author?"

"The romance author that had her book turned into a movie a few years ago, and Jolie was in the movie. That's why I recognized your name!"

"How do you know that?" Jeannie asked, looking at Ellie.

"It was in *PEOPLE* magazine."

"Your bible," Jeannie said. "Got it."

"Yeah, can we not make a fuss about it?" I asked with a hopeful smile.

"But it's a big deal! Did you go to the set? Did you get a say in casting? What was it like?"

"Boundaries, Ellie," Jeannie said. "We don't want to scare Sibby out of town. How are you liking Gator Springs?"

I breathed a sigh of relief as Jeannie threw me a bone. "So far, I'm loving it. Everyone's been really friendly."

"Friendly," Ellie repeated. "You mean Luke?"

I frowned. "Of course, Luke. He's Aunt Ida's attorney."

"I heard he picked you up from the airport," Jeannie said.

"He's very handsome," Ellie added.

I held up my hand and showed them my ring. "I'm happily married. With seven-year-old twins."

Ellie sighed. "He needs a nice girl."

"Nice and single," I reiterated. "So, uh, can you tell me some things about Aunt Ida? She and I are distantly related, but I didn't know her well."

"She used to come in every other Saturday to get her hair done," Jeannie said.

"So, you knew her well?"

"Very."

"What was she like?" I asked.

"Ida was eccentric," Ellie said. "Never married. Liked strays. People as well as animals."

"Everyone loved her," Jeannie added. "She was always willing to lend a hand or her time. She organized a lot of town events. She was at the front and center of everything in Gator Springs."

"A real social butterfly, but genuine," Ellie added.

"She traveled alone a lot. Took road trips in that pink Cadillac. Sometimes, she'd just take off in the middle of the night and I'd get a phone call in the morning and she'd be in another state."

"She loved the Ozarks," Ellie said.

Jeannie grinned. "And the Alamo."

Nodding, I set the magazine down and stood up. "It was nice meeting you. I'm going to head out."

"Come back soon," Jeannie said.

"I will, thanks."

"Hello?" I croaked into my cell.

"Hi," Aidan greeted. "You were asleep."

I wiped a hand down my face. "Yup."

"It's seven thirty," he said with a chuckle.

"I hung out on the beach today and my afternoon nap turned into an evening nap."

"Did you buy a bathing suit?"

"In a manner of speaking," I said.

"What's that mean?"

"It means I bought a one piece with big purple flowers on it, more designed to appeal to the older crowd. I had to buy a cover up to cover it up. At least I didn't burn."

He chuckled. "Remind me to grab your suit for you before I head down."

"Ah, good thinking."

"So, you played in the sand and took a nap. Learn anything about Aunt Ida?"

"A bit." I told him about my morning at the salon. "It doesn't feel like I know anything real about her though. I'll talk to more people in town. Hopefully with enough stories, she'll become real to me and not just some distant relative. Did I tell you the attic is full of boxes and scrapbooks?"

"No."

"I've started going through some things but there's some heavy stuff I'll need your help with."

"You mean you're just waiting to use me for my brawn?"

"Yeah. You okay with that?"

"Completely. So, have you caused any trouble yet?"

"What do you mean have I caused any trouble yet?"

"Well, it's you. And I've got to play the odds, you know?"

"I'm offended."

"No, you're not."

"You're right. I'm not. But I will have you know that I have not set anything on fire or backed the car into anything. My powers of destruction have gone dormant for the time being. There's also no trouble for me to get into here." I paused for a moment and then said, "Alex called me."

"Did you answer?"

"Yes."

"And?"

"I told her to back off."

"And what did she say?"

"I give it a week before she's back to begging me to write another romance novel."

He fell silent for a moment. "Can I ask you something?"

"Of course."

"Why *haven't* you written another romance?"

"I'm focusing on the children's books with Nat."

"Yeah. I know. But you love writing romance. Has that changed?"

"No. You remember what we went through after the movie with Jolie."

"You needed a break. I know. It's just…well, it's been a few years. When does a break become a permanent hiatus?"

"Not you too," I groaned.

"I'm not pressuring you. You know I'm not. But I'd hate for you not to be writing something you love just because you're worried about being thrust back into the spotlight again."

"You've never said any of this before," I said. "Why are you saying it now?"

"Because I think you're ready to hear it. And I think

you want to write another love story even if you aren't admitting it to yourself."

I didn't reply as I pondered his words.

"Sib? You okay?"

"Yeah. I'm fine."

"I better go. Caleb and I have a meeting with some Canadian investors."

"Good luck," I said.

"Thanks. Love you."

"Love you too."

After hanging up, I went into the kitchen and grabbed a glass of water. Then I made sure the house was locked up before heading upstairs. I got to the master bedroom and turned the knob, but the door refused to open. I pushed against it, fiddling with the handle, but the door remained steadfastly shut, as if someone had locked it from the inside.

"This is nuts," I muttered.

I knocked. "Do you mind opening this door? I'd like to go to sleep."

As soon as I uttered the words the door sprang open. I stood at the threshold, gathering the courage to step into the room.

Something really freakin' weird was going on here.

It began to rain while I was brushing my teeth and getting ready for bed. Storms, as a general rule, didn't scare me. Even my children were not the type to wake up in the middle of the night and climb into bed with Aidan and me.

But this storm felt ominous and eerie. Maybe because I was already on edge. I fell asleep, but it was fitful, and I never sank completely into unconsciousness.

A sound jarred me awake, but I wasn't sure what it was. I clutched the quilt to me as I listened for a moment. I heard nothing aside from thick, heavy raindrops smacking against the glass windows.

I flung the covers off and turned on the lamp resting on the bedside table. I threw on a sweater and a thick pair of socks and then traipsed downstairs. Luckily, all the lights turned on when I flicked their switches, so that calmed my racing heart a bit.

But when I was in the kitchen filling the tea kettle, I swore I heard a groan. When a rogue branch dropped onto the roof, I let out a squeal of surprise.

"Get a grip, Sibby," I said.

Just when my heart rate returned to normal, the doorbell rang.

"Gah!"

I looked at the clock on the microwave. It was just past one in the morning and there was no reason for anyone to be ringing my doorbell.

Ergo, I deduced I really did have a ghost and it liked to play games.

"Hello! Is anyone home?"

I looked around for something to use to defend myself. Some crazy criminal was standing on the threshold of my doorstep, waiting to see if anyone was home before charging in and ransacking the place. I was sure of it.

I grabbed the potato masher and brandished it like a sword. I wasn't exactly sure how I was going to defend myself with it, but I felt better armed with it than without. I crept toward the front door, wishing I hadn't left my cell phone upstairs.

"Sibby!" the voice called again, followed by incessant knocking.

Huh. The criminal knew my name.

"Who's there!" I called out.

"Jolie! Let me in! I'm getting drenched!"

I hastily ran to the door and unlocked it.

Jolie Kingston stood on the front porch, drenched from head to toe. Her mascara was running, and her hair was plastered to her neck and cheeks.

She blinked. "Is that a potato masher?"

"Yes," I said, lowering it immediately. "Come in. How did you know I was here? And why are you here? Do you know what time it is?"

Jolie stepped inside, droplets of water pooling on the floor. "I talked to your husband earlier. He didn't mention it?"

"No. But I talked to him around seven thirty and then went back to bed."

I shut the front door wand waved her toward the kitchen.

"Went *back* to bed?" she asked.

"I was in the sun most of the day and I forgot how it takes it out of you." I gestured with my thumb. "The beach is literally five hundred feet that way."

"You're kidding."

"Nope. Stay right there. I'm going to get you a towel."

"Thanks."

There were several beach towels in the laundry room just off the kitchen. I took a couple, just in case, and headed back into the foyer.

Jolie had already removed her shoes and socks, but she was still in her wet jeans and white T-shirt. The straps of her red bra showed through.

"Suitcase?"

"In the car." She looked forlornly at the front door. "I guess I should run out and grab it?"

"I have some spare sweats if you want."

"I want," she said eagerly. "Thanks."

I ran up the stairs and found a pair of gray sweats and

one of Aidan's T-shirts. I brought them back downstairs and handed them to Jolie.

"You mind if I change right here?"

"Go for it."

She peeled off her soggy clothes and donned the baggy sweats and shirt.

"Want some tea?" I asked.

"Sure." She followed me into the kitchen and then sat down at the table. "Sorry to just show up, but I did text you. So, I technically did give you a heads up."

"My phone has been on silent," I said. "Not that I'm not happy to see you, but it's late at night and—"

"And why am I here?" she asked.

"Yeah."

"Had a break from filming," she said. "And I wanted to get out of dodge for a bit."

"Hmmm."

"What do you mean, *hmmm*?"

"I mean, something smells fishy, and it isn't this beach town. Where's the show filming again? Greenpoint, right?"

"Yeah."

"So, you just hopped on a plane from New York and came down here? It's a forty-five-minute drive from the airport. How did you get here? Cab?"

"Couldn't get a cab so I bought a car from someone at the airport. It's parked out front of your house."

"You *bought* a car?" I repeated. "Seriously?"

"Like I said, none of the cabs would take me to Gator Springs so I walked the parking lots for a few minutes and found a guy about to drive home. Made him a deal. He's going to mail me the title in a couple of days. Don't worry about it. And what's with the third degree?"

"The third degree? It's one in the morning and you

show up drenched from head to toe out of the blue. I think I'm entitled to some answers, no?"

"Window on the car is broken and it started raining. You're not happy to see me?"

"Of course I'm happy to see you. I'm even happier that you weren't a ghost."

"I don't understand."

I sighed. "I'm pretty sure this house is haunted."

Chapter 8

JOLIE DIDN'T EVEN BAT an eye when I explained the weirdness that had been occurring in Aunt Ida's house. She nodded along like it was a viable explanation.

"Everyone knows that if a house is haunted, you have to smudge it, tell the ghost to go to the other side, and get a guardian gnome."

"What's a guardian gnome? Is this like some weird, Hollywood new-age fad?"

"Make fun of me if you want, but my home is guarded by a gnome, and I don't have any ghosts."

"Will you help me banish the ghost tomorrow?"

"Sure thing."

"I think the rain has mostly stopped. Do you need help with your luggage?"

"Nah. I just brought a small bag with me. I'll grab it."

The tea kettle began to whistle, and I got up from the table.

"I'll be back," Jolie announced.

While she was getting her luggage, I fixed us two cups

of tea. She came back a few moments later and then closed and locked the front door.

"Aidan tried to explain to me about your Aunt Ida, but I'm still confused on how you're related. She's not your actual aunt, is she?"

Jolie sat down at the table, and I slid a mug toward her.

"A cousin of a sort," I said. "I have no idea why she named me her heir. I didn't even know her. I met her when I was a kid apparently, though I have no recollection of that. According to the townsfolk, she was eccentric."

"The townsfolk?" she asked with a smile.

"It seemed appropriate." I sighed. "Why couldn't I have inherited a house that wasn't haunted? I mean, it would've made things a lot easier."

"Ghosts aren't the problem. Banshees, on the other hand... I once stayed at a haunted castle in Ireland. Trust me, Southern ghosts have nothing on Irish banshees."

"I'll take your word for it." I took my mug of tea and waved her toward the direction of the stairs. "You can have your pick of rooms. But I don't suggest the creepy doll room."

"There's a creepy doll room?"

"Yup. I need to change that pronto. Even the thought of them living in the same house with me gives me the sheekie-heebies."

"The what?"

"Sorry, I meant the heebie-jeebies. Oliver calls them the sheekie-heebies."

"Cute."

I turned off the downstairs lights and then we headed up to the second floor. Jolie set down her suitcase and extended the handle.

"Show me a non-creepy room."

I took her to the room across from the master and

opened the door. I flipped on the light. "The sheets are clean, and there's a bathroom down that way," I pointed to the opposite end of the hallway.

"Thanks," she said. "This is great."

"I'm really glad you randomly showed up," I said to her. "It's strange being here by myself. I haven't been alone in a long time. It's nice having company."

"You just want my help getting rid of your ghost."

"In exchange for room and board," I teased.

"Done and done. I'll help you get rid of your ghost tomorrow."

"Stop laughing, it's not funny," I said.

"It's pretty funny," Aidan said and then he started to laugh again. "I can picture it. You having just woken up, defending yourself with a potato masher. Priceless."

"If there had been a cast-iron frying pan, I would've armed myself with that."

"How long is she staying?" he asked.

"No idea. She didn't say. I assume a few days. She'll have to get back to filming." I fell silent for a moment and then I asked, "It's kind of strange, though, right? I mean she just showed up randomly late at night? Like why did she come here? She's rich. She could've gone anywhere for a break, but she chose this place, with me."

"Ask her."

"I will. She was kind of evasive last night. Or maybe I was too surprised to see her to really press the issue. I don't know, it's just bizarre."

I sniffed the air. I smelled coffee. Jolie was already awake. How was that even possible?

"Can I switch gears?" he asked.

"Go for it."

"I was thinking, I'll be done with the brew festival in a couple days. I can head down with the dog, and then in a few weeks when Mom and Dad are finished with their national park trip, they could drive to Gator Springs in the motorhome and stay for a bit. We can have an end of summer bash, and then you, me, the kids, the dog can road trip back to New York."

I thought for a moment. "That means you and I would be down here for several weeks, just hanging out."

"You don't want to hang out with me? Just the two of us?" he teased.

"Oh stop," I said with a laugh. "It'll be like olden times when it was just you, me, and the dog. Think Annie and Caleb can sneak away from all their adulting to come hang out with us too?"

"I'll ask Caleb."

"Perfect," I said with a wide grin. "We can boil sea food and you can bury me in the sand."

"You really want me to bury you in the sand?"

"No, but I'm not really good at building sandcastles, so I thought being buried in the sand is a viable alternative."

"Weirdo," he said with a laugh.

"You mind if I let you go? Jolie already made coffee and I'm dying for my bean juice. That's the one of the things sorely lacking down here. Good coffee. There's not even a decent cafe."

"Annie could open a restaurant down there and it would probably do really well."

"She'd have to learn how to cook gator."

"She always did love a good challenge. Love you, Sib. Talk to you later."

I tossed my phone onto the bed and then stood up. I was dragging just a little bit due to the erratic sleep last night.

I headed downstairs and into the kitchen. Jolie sat at the table, her blonde hair pulled into a side pony tail. Her cornflower blue eyes skimmed over me and she smirked.

"How do you look like that first thing in the morning?" I demanded.

"Look like what?"

"Like a Disney princess who never suffers from lack of sleep."

"My secret? Thick under eye concealer."

"So, you're not perfect?"

"Nope. I'm usually airbrushed."

"Thank God you're human. I was worried for a second."

She grinned. "Did the scent of coffee pull you from a deep slumber in your cave?"

"You know it. I'm a mother of seven-year-old twins. Coffee is life."

Jolie snorted. "Are there any good breakfast places in this town?"

"Hmm. Bob's might serve breakfast. Not really sure."

"Bob's?"

"It's the only place in town that serves food, but it's more of a bar. A tiki bar, actually."

"You're kidding."

"Oh, I wish that I was. The floor is covered in sand."

She uncurled her legs from beneath her, and her sock-clad feet hit the linoleum. "What are we waiting for? We need to go. I have to see this place right now."

I held up my hand. "Not before I have at least one cup of coffee. And…"

"And?" she prodded.

"This is a small town, and everyone in the world knows your face."

"Not *everyone*," she said with a laugh.

"Fine. Ninety percent at least."

"We'll just tell people I'm your good friend from New York and I'll go by my given name."

"Jolie isn't your given name?"

"No. It's my middle name. My real name is actually Brenda."

"Huh. I never knew that."

She shrugged. "So, we can go out and about and you can show me the town just as long as you remember to call me Brenda."

"Yeah, we could do that," I said slowly. "But even without airbrushing, you still look like you. You're still recognizable."

"So what? I'll go by Brenda, and if people tell me I look like that celebrity Jolie Kingston, I'll tell them I get that all the time."

"The woman who owns the salon—which is the Gator Springs equivalent of the local news station—knows that I know you."

"How?"

"There was a magazine with your face on it. It was a topic of conversation. I accidentally let it slip that I knew you."

She blinked and then shook her head. "So, let's steer

clear of the salon. I'm not going to be a shut-in while I'm here."

"And that's another thing. How long are you staying? You never did say."

"A few days," she replied. "Maybe a week. Is that okay?"

"Of course it's okay," I assured her. "But until Aidan gets down here to help me with the attic, I need a helper."

"No sweat."

"Okay, so we'll have breakfast at Bob's, then I'll show you Main Street, then—"

"Then the beach," she begged.

"The beach." I nodded.

"What are we doing for dinner?"

"We haven't had breakfast yet and you're already thinking about dinner?" I asked in amusement.

"I'm on vacation. I'm going to live a little."

Chapter 9

TWENTY MINUTES LATER, I was locking up the house. Jolie stood next to me, her hair pulled into a ponytail. She wore only a bit of mascara and lip gloss.

I glared at her.

"What?" she demanded.

"Did you use any hair product?"

"No."

"Really? Your hair looks like *that* in this humidity? If you weren't so effing down to earth and genuine, I'd hate you a little bit."

"I think your frizzy hair is adorable," she commented.

"So, you've noticed it?"

"Well, yeah, I've noticed it. Kind of hard not to."

"At least I know you'll never lie to me," I said.

"Never. You have no idea how hard it is to find people to tell you the truth." She paused, looking sad and thoughtful at the same time.

"You okay?" I asked quietly.

"Me?" She tossed her head, reminding me of a spirited horse. "I'm perfect."

"Listen, I know you're a professional actor for a living, but I don't buy that you're *perfect*."

"No?"

"You came here late last night, and it seems like it was on a…whim."

"It was a bit impulsive," she admitted. "But I realized I hadn't seen you in months and I had some free time, so…"

"Well, it's good to see you. Seriously." I stepped down off the porch steps but came to an immediate halt.

"What the hell is that?" I demanded.

"I told you I bought a car," she explained.

"Yeah, but I thought you'd done some crazy celebrity crap and bought a Mercedes or Hummer or something. Not *that*."

That in question was a rusted-out twenty-year-old Honda Civic with chipped paint, a broken driver side window, and a missing hub cap. And that was just what I could see from a quick glance.

"How did that car even make it from the airport to Gator Springs?"

"It was touch and go," she admitted. "I think it needs a new muffler. Or an oil change. Or a new engine…"

"Or D, all of the above."

"You really didn't hear me drive up last night? I swore I woke the town."

"That thing needs to make its way to a junk yard, pronto. It's a hazard."

"I don't plan on driving it again," she said. "You have a car here, right? Aidan said something about a pink Cadillac?"

"Mint condition," I said with a wide grin. "With an old radio still in it."

"Get out."

"Nope. Maybe we'll take a drive in it later tonight with the top down and find a drive-in with hamburgers and milkshakes."

"You really do want to live in the fifties, don't you?"

"I don't think I'd mind. Running after ice cream trucks, riding your bike outside your house." I sighed. "Those were the days."

"Yeah, you weren't alive then, so why are you sighing for the nostalgia of the times?"

"I'm a writer, it's what we do."

"You mean you play make believe and create worlds from your mind."

"That too."

We headed in the direction of town.

"Speaking of writing… What are you working on right now?" she asked.

"Nothing, actually."

"Seriously?"

"Seriously."

"Not even mindless scribbles?" she asked.

"Not even those."

"Doesn't seem like you," she said.

"What does seem like me?" I inquired.

"I dunno. You're always moving and grooving on some creative endeavor."

"I'm just enjoying life, you know? Sometimes that's enough."

I said it, but a niggling worry sprouted in the back of my mind. Writing romance was part of my roots. It's what I wanted to do all those years ago when I was a waitress and my life had become a dumpster fire.

Maybe I had turned my back on it. Maybe it had been easier to walk away, to shut it down, than to continue after such monumental success. A part of me had really loved building something else from scratch. There had been no pressure to do well. I'd just written a children's book for fun, and it had turned into its own thing.

Now, it might be time to get back to writing romance. I wouldn't tell anyone though. Not until there was something to tell.

"You forgot my mug," Norm said.

I winced. "I took good care of it. It's at home in the dish drain. I'll bring it back, I swear."

"She's good for her word," Jolie said, plopping her bottom down on the stool next to me.

Norm frowned at Jolie and then looked back to me. "I thought you came to Gator Springs alone."

"This is my friend...Brenda." I stumbled over her introduction, but Norm didn't notice, thank goodness. "She surprised me. Now we're having a girls' week of relaxation."

"Hey, don't ignore us," Ralph said, lifting a cup of coffee to his lips.

"Right, sorry. Ralph, Bill, and Oscar."

"Nice to meet you boys," Jolie quipped.

Oscar cocked his head to the side. "You look familiar."

"Do I?" Jolie asked, batting her lashes.

"Yeah." Ralph nodded, resembling a bobbing chicken head. "You look like someone."

"She looks like herself," I said quickly. "Good 'ole Brenda."

"Smooth," Jolie said out of the corner of her mouth.

"We'll have two breakfast specials," I said. "And we'll take them over there." I pointed to the table in the corner.

"Why can't we sit here at the bar?" Jolie asked.

"I don't like to eat food when my feet aren't touching the floor," I lied. I just didn't want the Hawaiian shirt crew to eavesdrop on our conversation.

"You're a weirdo," Jolie said.

"Says the woman who believes in guardian gnomes."

"What's a guardian gnome?" Norm asked.

Jolie opened her mouth, but before she could get a word in edge wise, I said, "A gnome statue that lives outside your house in your front yard and adds a little pizzazz to your garden."

"Isn't that just a regular garden gnome?" Ralph asked.

"Yes, exactly," I said.

"I don't get it," Oscar muttered.

"Is there a plant store in town?" Jolie asked.

"Bendel's Nursery," Oscar said. "Just outside of town."

"Awesome." Jolie reached for a laminated menu and flipped it over. "There's a raccoon on the back of this menu."

"That's Bob," I explained.

"Bob?" Jolie raised her brows. "You mean the bar was named after a raccoon."

"Yup." I nodded.

"God, I love this place," Jolie said.

"Please don't tell people about it," Bill said. "We want to keep this little town little."

"Got it." Jolie mimed zipping her lips and throwing away the key.

The front door to the bar opened and Ellie strode in.

"Hey, Ellie." Ralph looked over at her. "Did you get a haircut?"

Ellie primped her grayish bob. "I did."

"It looks nice."

"Thank you," she said, her cheeks turning pink.

Jolie elbowed me and nodded with her chin, a smile on her lips.

Middle-aged love in Gator Springs, Florida. Kind of adorable.

Ellie's gaze slid from Ralph to me and then to Jolie. "You look familiar."

"That's what I said," Ralph said.

"You look just like Jolie Kingston," Ellie announced. She leaned forward to study Jolie at closer range.

"Wow, if I had a nickel," Jolie drawled. "My name's Brenda. Breeennnnndaaaa."

"Norm, I'm getting hungry," I said. "How about those breakfast specials?"

"Sure thing," Norm said, knocking his knuckles against the bar. "Ellie, are you staying?"

"I'll stay for a cup of coffee."

Ellie kept giving Jolie the side eye, even as she plunked down on a stool near Ralph.

Breakfast was simple and gator free. I quickly paid the check, promised to bring Norm's mug back, and then ushered Jolie out the door.

"That was fun," Jolie said as we stepped outside. She lowered her sunglasses onto her eyes. "I was surprised by how good the food was."

"Yeah, I've only eaten there twice, but so far I've enjoyed it."

"Tell me how you feel about this," Jolie said. "I was thinking we could hit Bendel's Nursery and grab a gnome. Then maybe walk on the beach and then later tonight I can help you in the attic."

"You just want to ride in the pink Cadillac."

"Can I drive it?"

"Hell no," I said.

"I get the point of one guardian gnome," I said as I closed the trunk of the convertible. "But three?"

"They work better as triplets," she said. "Trust me."

"I bow to your wisdom."

She held up the gnome with a blue hat and a pipe. "This one sits between us on the ride home."

"You've been living in LA too long. You've gotten Hollyweird."

I unlocked the car and then slid into the front seat. I waited until Jolie was buckled in and then I slowly backed out of Bendel's Nursery.

"He looks like a Bilius," I said.

"Who?"

I gestured with my chin to the gnome.

She grinned. "Someone's been watching Harry Potter."

"I won't deny it."

"Let's take the scenic route. Bilius should see the sights."

We were bopping along to oldies when Jolie suddenly screamed, "Sibby!"

"Crap!" I yelled, swerving off the road so I didn't hit the giant alligator that had appeared from nowhere.

Unfortunately, that meant driving into the ditch. I threw my arm out in front of Bilius and Jolie.

My arm smacked into Jolie's breastbone even as the car came to a stop. "Sorry, soccer mom reflexes."

"Your kids don't play soccer," she said, rubbing her sternum.

"It's an expression. Are you okay?"

"Yeah. I'm okay. What about you?"

"Fine." I looked behind me. The gator looked really close. It lifted its head to the sky and then scuttled toward the car.

"We have to get out of here. I do not want to turn into a gator snack," I said.

The ditch was still muddy from the previous night's rainstorm, so I sent a prayer to Moses and pressed on the gas. I breathed a sigh of relief when the Caddy got back onto the asphalt without a problem.

"Luke warned me about deer in the road, not gators," I said, gripping the steering wheel.

"We're just outside of Gator Springs. Gators make sense," Jolie said. "Who's Luke?"

"Aunt Ida's lawyer. He picked me up from the airport."

She started to laugh. "Oh man, can you imagine what

would've happened if we'd hit that thing? I'm pretty sure we would've been run out of town."

I looked in the rearview mirror as I put the car into drive. I could still see the beast. It hadn't yet fully crossed the road.

"Is that—yeah, there's a giant white stripe down its back. Have you ever seen anything like that?" I asked.

"Never. Then again, I've never seen an alligator crossing the road. Deer, yes. Sheep, yes. Bear, yes. Even an armadillo and a tortoise. But never an alligator."

Chapter 10

"Bash told me you guys talked a few weeks ago," Jolie said as she set a cup of tea down in front of me.

"Yeah, we talked," I said.

"Are you and Aidan going to Scotland for Em's surprise birthday party?"

"Yup. You? Will you be able to get away from your crazy schedule?"

"Yeah, I think I'll be able to swing it." She sat down and grabbed her own mug of tea. "I can't believe Bash has procreated. He was my first on-screen kiss. Did you know that?"

"No, I didn't know. Fun Jolie Kingston trivia."

Bash Hamilton and Jolie had starred in a movie together when they'd both been fresh faces on the Hollywood scene. They'd remained good friends after filming.

By some weird twist of fate, Em and Bash had once gone to acting camp together and they'd reconnected after Caleb had left her at the altar. Now Em and Bash were married, had a kid, and were living in Scotland. Not too shabby, even though Em's happily ever after hadn't come easily.

"Mini Bash is adorable," I said.

"Really adorable," she agreed. "Wow, everyone I know has children. Wacky."

"Huh, I just realized, you're actually my only friend who doesn't have kids."

"What about the friend that is engaged to the chef? Stacy?"

"You remember Stacy?"

"The PR marketing genius, of course I remember her. I talked to her at your housewarming for a while."

I nodded. "Right. I forgot you've met her."

When we'd finished renovating the house Upstate, we'd invited all our friends to a housewarming. The house had been full of friends, neighbors, and family.

"Yeah, Stacy is actually pregnant and about to become one of those chic Parisian moms. She and Gregory moved to France a year ago so he could open a restaurant. She's handling PR for him."

"Exciting times," she said. "So, speaking of house-warmings… I might've bought you a present at Bendels' Nursery while you were looking at gnomes."

"You already got the smudging stuff. What else did you get?"

She grinned and pulled out a plastic bag from her pocket and threw it on the table in front of me. "Bendel has another type of plant, way, way in the back, but you have to ask for it…"

I frowned. "I don't understand. What is that?"

"Pot, Sibby. Bendel grows pot."

"Pot!"

"Why do you sound so scandalized?" she asked with a grin.

"I don't smoke. It makes me loopy."

"That's the point. Come on, what do you say?"

"Wow, peer pressure much?" I teased.

"We're in a house, we're safe. We're not driving anywhere. What's the worst that could happen? Live a little, Sibby. Also, Ouija boards are way more fun when you're stoned. Trust me."

"I don't have an Ouija board."

She grinned. "I found Aunt Ida's board game closet. She has like, the *original* Monopoly and an old Ouija board from who knows when."

"Ouija boards? Everyone knows they don't work," I said.

"So, by that logic if they don't work then you're not afraid to try it out?"

"Nope. I'm not scared at all."

Jolie plucked a joint from the baggie. "I figured we could get high and ask the ghost who it is and what it wants."

"I'm insane to even entertain this idea. Okay. I'm in. But if my husband calls, don't let me say anything stupid."

"No promises."

We set up the Ouija board in front of the unlit fireplace and then placed pillows on the rug to make a huge pile.

"I'm suddenly craving Moroccan food," I commented.

"You're supposed to have the food cravings *after* you smoke. That's the rule."

Jolie grabbed the lighter from the mantle and after a few minutes we were both feeling chill from our herbal infusion. "You ready to do this Ouija board?"

"Let's do it."

We both placed our hands on the planchette.

"Now what?" I asked.

"Now we ask a question," she said.

"Is there a ghost in this house?" I asked jokingly.

My smile slipped as the planchette began to move and went immediately to the *yes* text on the board.

I looked at Jolie with unease.

"Ask another question," she urged.

I nodded. "What's your name?"

The planchette slid across the board. First to the R, then the A, then the Y.

"Ray," Jolie said. "Who's Ray?"

She'd asked me the question, but apparently Ray's spirit was moved to answer the question because the planchette glided across the board.

"I-D-A-S-L-O-V-E-R." I frowned. "Ida's lover. Ida's *lover*? No one in town said anything about Ida having a lover."

"This is getting weird," she muttered. "Either this pot is really freakin' strong, or this shit is for real."

"I don't know about you, but I'm hoping it's the pot."

"Ask another question. Something not related to Ida and Ray."

"Okay."

When I didn't voice a question right away, she said, "Go on."

"I'm thinking! This is important." I bit my lip. "Okay. I got one. Should I write another romance—"

Goodbye.

I lifted my hands from the planchette. "Ouija boards are stupid."

"Very stupid," she said slowly.

"I don't believe in them."

"Nope. I don't either."

I sighed. "Give me that joint. I need another toke."

"You're a ridiculous human, and I love you."

"What was that last question you were asking Ray?" Jolie inquired from a sprawled position on the couch.

"Hmm?" I was supine on the floor, my face and tail-bone numb, but with no intention of moving.

"You were asking Ray a question about writing. Or you were going to until he signed off."

"Yeah, he totally ghosted us. The ghost ghosted me."

"So?"

"So? So what?"

"What were you asking him?"

"It doesn't matter," I said, changing the conversation. "I'm curious about Ray. Who was he? What did he look like? When was he with Ida? Have you noticed there are no personal photographs in the house? It's weird. There are photo albums up in the attic. Maybe they'll shed some light on this mysterious Ray."

Jolie peeled herself off the couch.

"I'm not in the frame of mind to search right now," I said to her.

"Good, I'm just going to the bathroom."

While she was gone, I didn't move from the floor. I was comfortable, and I was just about to doze off when the doorbell rang.

I groaned. What was it about small towns where people just randomly showed up at your door?

There was no way to pretend I wasn't home. Even though the Cadillac was in the garage and it was closed, Jolie's beater was still out front.

I went to answer the door, making sure to peer through the peephole first.

Betty Sue. Carrying another casserole dish.

How many of those did she have to spare?

I opened the door. "Betty Sue," I greeted. "How nice to see you."

Her hair was in perfect pin curls and her polka dotted dress flared out into a wide skirt. She looked ready to attend a 1950s cocktail party. I wondered if she made a good Old Fashioned.

"I brought you another dish," she said. "How did you like the gator frittata?"

"Excellent," I admitted truthfully. "I demolished it."

She sniffed the air. "Were you cooking? Is that oregano?"

"Uh, just burned some incense," I lied.

Jolie bounded down the stairs, her cell phone clutched in her hand. She paused at the bottom of the steps.

Betty Sue's mouth dropped open but then she quickly recovered. "Hello. I heard Sibby had a house guest, but I…"

Jolie feigned an innocent expression. "But?"

"Well, it's just that you look *exactly* like Jolie Kingston," Betty Sue finished.

"I get that a lot. My name is Brenda," Jolie said, repeating the party line. "Love your dress."

"Er—thank you." Betty Sue preened. "I brought another dish. Crawdad casserole."

"Thank you. Smells great," I said.

"And I'm famished," Jolie said.

Betty Sue handed me the glassware. "There's a beat-up old car outside your house."

"It's mine," Jolie said.

"Ah," Betty Sue said.

Awkward silence fell over the foyer.

"Oh, right. Let me get you your clean dish." I quickly went to the kitchen and placed the crawdad casserole on the stove and grabbed the glass from the dish drain.

Jolie was fielding questions from Betty Sue, but I wasn't worried about it. Jolie was a professional actress and she'd spent years learning how to dodge questions she didn't want to answer.

"Here you go," I announced, handing over the casserole dish to Betty Sue. "Thanks again for stopping by."

"I was just telling your friend that we have a local book club. Friday is my turn to host, and we'd love it if you joined us," Betty Sue said. "I know it's sort of last minute and you don't even have to read the book. Just come and join us for girl chat and a glass of wine."

"That's so nice of you to invite us," I said. "We'll see if we can make it."

Betty Sue frowned. "Oh."

"We're in. Sounds fun," Jolie said.

"Wonderful! I'll let you get back to it." She sniffed the air. "I just love that incense you were using, what's the name of—."

"Thanks again! Bye!" I waved at her and shut the door behind her, and for good measure, I locked it. I whirled on Jolie. "Why the hell did you promise her we'd come to her book club meeting?"

"Because she was never going to leave otherwise," Jolie said. "That woman is like all kinds of fake nice."

"Hmm. Yeah, I'm not sure I buy the bubbly act. Bet she's got a streak of darkness."

"Like kinky darkness?"

"What? Ew. No."

"You're right. There's no way she'd do anything to ruin her perfect curls."

"Luke said that Betty Sue has wanted this house for years and she's going to probably make me an offer on it."

"Know your enemies, huh?"

"I'm not her enemy."

"No? You're just standing in the way of her getting this house. Why does she want it, anyway?"

"I think she wants to turn into a bed and breakfast." I shrugged.

"Well, I've never been one to turn down free food. What do you say we eat that crawdad thing and then smudge the entire house? With sage this time…"

Chapter 11

"Sibby," Jolie whispered. "Sibby, wake up!"

I moaned. "What's wrong?"

"Nothing."

"Then why are you waking me up?" I pulled the pillow over my head.

"I'm going to meditate on the beach."

"Good for you. Go away."

"Come with me."

"No."

"Sibby, come on, it'll be good for you."

"Sleep is also good for you. You're supposed to get eight hours, but I've never subscribed to that. I need a solid nine. And I've been sleep deprived for years because of my children."

"So? You won't catch up in one night."

I sighed and tossed my pillow aside. "What time is it?"

"5:45."

"You are evil."

"I've got coffee brewing."

"You still must be destroyed," I muttered, but I threw

the comforter off my body and planted my feet onto the floor.

"I'll be downstairs," she said as she retreated from the room.

I turned on the bedside lamp so I could see better. I stumbled to the bathroom and splashed some cold water on my face.

I slipped into yoga pants, a tank top, and a hoodie. It was cool on the beach before the sun came up.

Jolie was already drinking a cup of coffee when I came downstairs.

Without a word, I poured myself a cup and added a heavy splash of cream. I was dragging so hard. We'd stayed up late and tried to Ouija board again, but Ray hadn't come through, making me think we'd made it all up to begin with.

I'd brought down a pair of tube socks and I put them on, followed by my old pair of tennis shoes before following Jolie. She carried two bath towels. When we got to the beach, she spread them out onto the sand.

"I wish we had yoga mats," she said.

An hour later, Jolie was jostling me awake. The sun was aloft, and the smell of the sea was in my nose.

"What happened?" I slurred.

"You tried to meditate, and you fell asleep."

She was grinning at me.

I slowly sat up and stared at the waves that rolled up the beach. "Jeez, have you ever been to a more peaceful place?"

"I did a yoga retreat in Costa Rica," Jolie said.

I rolled my eyes at her.

"But this is a pretty close second," she admitted. "I need to use the bathroom. And then I want to shower and have more coffee."

"I want a few more minutes on the beach."

Only when my butt grew numb did I stand up. I stretched my arms over my head and then picked up my towel. When I walked into the kitchen, my phone was buzzing across the table. Aside from Aidan, I wasn't sure who would be calling me this early.

It wasn't Aidan, but my mother.

"Oy, I don't have the energy for this right now." I silenced the call and set my phone aside. My phone buzzed after a moment, letting me know I had a voicemail.

I headed upstairs and took a fast shower. When I returned to the kitchen, it was still empty and Jolie was nowhere to be found. I didn't bother listening to my mother's voicemail, I just called her back.

"Good morning," she chirped.

"You're happy," I remarked.

"Why wouldn't I be happy? The sun is shining, your father and I played a round of golf, and we're getting a couple's massage later today, which will no doubt lead to sex—"

"You know what? I don't need the details," I interrupted. "I'm returning your call. So, what's up?"

"How are things in Gator Springs?"

"Good," I said. "The house is incredible, a hop skip and a jump away from the beach. Actually, you and dad should come down. We want to have an end of summer bash before heading back to New York."

"Oh! What a fun idea. I'll talk to your father, but I'm sure we can make the trip. Are you—do you think you're keeping the house?"

"Aidan and I haven't officially decided anything, but I think so." I bit my lip. "Mom? Did you know if Aunt Ida had any boyfriends?"

"I don't know much about Ida's personal life. She kept to herself. *Bubbe* might know, though."

Jolie walked into the kitchen, freshly scrubbed and clean. Her blonde hair was pulled back away from her face, and she suddenly looked very young and innocent.

"I'll ask her when she finally docks."

My grandparents were currently on a cruise with Mrs. Nowaki and Jesse.

"Why are you wondering if Ida had boyfriends?" Mom asked.

"Just trying to get a sense of who she was," I said evasively.

"Hmm. Are you lonely being down there by yourself?"

"I was lonely," I admitted. "But Jolie came for a visit."

"Jolie? Jolie's there?"

"She surprised me," I remarked. "Now we're hanging out for a girls' week."

"Well, you tell that nice young woman I said hello and that I can't wait for her show to return for the fall season. That cliffhanger was—"

"Don't tell me! I haven't watched her show yet."

"You haven't watched it yet?" Jolie hissed.

I waved my hand at her. "Mom? I'll talk to you later. Love you."

"I can't believe you haven't seen my show," Jolie said after I hung up.

"I have seven-year-old twins, and the moment I sit down, one of them needs something. Or the dryer beeps. Or Aidan wants me to try a new craft beer. Or I'm washing my hair." I grinned. "My Netflix watch list is insane."

"So, you haven't not watched it because you think I'm a shit actress?"

"Okay, look." I pointed my finger at her. "There's only

room in this house for one neurotic artist, and I already claim that title."

"I'm not neurotic," she rebutted. "I'm just suffering a lack of confidence at the moment. Not the same thing."

"You are a godsend," I said.

"Hey, I'm just up here because I hope we find a pirate's treasure map hidden behind a picture frame."

I grinned at her. "My entire life I've hoped for a *Goonies* expedition."

"Same," she said. "Where should we start first?"

"The painting leaning up against the far wall is as good a place as any," I said. I gingerly made my way through the stacks of boxes and erratic furniture.

I plucked a painting off the floor. "I don't know anything about art."

It was a landscape piece of the beach and Aunt Ida's house. I peered in the corner of the canvas to read the signature. "Ida painted this one."

"Did she?" Jolie looked closer at the painting. "That's cool. She was pretty good."

"Yeah. I wonder why it's up here. I think I'll hang it downstairs, right in the front room."

I handed Jolie the painting and she took it out of the attic. "I'm just leaning it against the wall out here," she called.

"Thanks!"

I picked up another painting. It was bright and vibrant, painted withs streaks of pinks and reds.

"What a nice flower," I said. "Jolie, what do you think of this?" When Jolie didn't say anything, I looked at her over my shoulder.

Her lips trembled and then she burst into laughter.

"What's so funny?"

"That's not a flower," she wheezed. "It's a——"

"Oh my God," I muttered. "It's a vagina!"

Jolie bent over, laughing so hard she began to wheeze.

"Well, I'm definitely not hanging this up in the house," I stated. "I have kids and they'll ask questions I'm not ready to answer."

"What's the signature in the corner? Another one of Ida's?"

"How would she have even painted this?"

"I dunno? A hand mirror?"

I glanced at the corner of the painting. "Ida didn't paint this."

"No?"

I looked at her. "Ray did."

"No way."

"Way. Man, I wish there was a last name on this thing."

The rest of the paintings were of Ida and there were several nudes, all done by the mysterious Ray.

This house just got wackier and wackier.

"What do you mean she still hasn't told you why she's there?" Annie asked.

"I mean, I haven't bugged her about it," I said, stirring the pasta noodles to make sure they didn't stick to the bottom of the pan.

"Maybe you should bug her about it," Annie groused. "Where is she now?"

"Out for a run on the beach."

Annie made a noise of frustration.

"What?" I demanded. "What's wrong with you?"

"Nothing's wrong with me."

"Annie."

"Sibby."

"Come on, tell me what's stuck in your craw."

"Nothing is stuck in my craw. What is a craw anyway?"

"I don't know. It's just something they say down here."

"You're not gonna like, up and move down there, are you?"

I set down the wooden spoon. "Why would you think I'd move down here?"

"I don't know. That's what you *do*."

"What do I do?"

"You up and change your life, so my life changes."

"Um, you were the one that sold your restaurant and moved Upstate."

"Yeah, I did," she admitted. "But only after you and Aidan left the city."

"You're being really weird. Did you drink coffee this morning?'

"Yes."

"So this isn't caffeine withdrawal?"

"No. It's not caffeine withdrawal."

"Then what is it?"

"You didn't even ask me to come down there with you!" she cried. "And now you're partying with Jolie."

"We're not partying. We're going through boxes in the attic."

"I can go through boxes in the attic…"

"Annie," I said. "You had shit on your plate. The Farmer's Market, and the new jam recipes, and Matilda, and—"

"You know I would've ditched all that stuff—I mean, not Matilda, obviously—for you. If you'd asked me."

"Didn't Caleb talk to you? About coming down at the end of summer?"

"Yeah, he talked to me about it," she said. "But meanwhile you and Jolie are smudging and buying gnomes and Ouija boarding and talking to ghosts."

"You make it sound like we're at sleepaway camp."

"You basically are. *And I'm not there.*"

The timer beeped. I used the wooden spoon to fish out a noodle and tasted it. They were done, so I turned off the stove.

"Are you even listening to me?" Annie screeched.

The back door opened as I was dumping the pot of noodles into the strainer over the sink.

"Yeah, I'm listening," I said. "Jolie just walked in, so unless you want her to hear your epic melt down, I suggest reining it in."

Annie hung up on me.

"What did I just walk into?" Jolie asked.

"I'm making dinner."

"Not that. Smells good, by the way."

I oiled the noodles so they wouldn't stick and then jumped back over to the stove to make sure the veggies were sautéing and not crisping.

"Annie's got her panties in a twist because you're down here with me and she's not."

"Did you tell her I randomly showed up and didn't even ask for an invite?"

I chuckled. "Yes."

"Did you tell her we're spending our time trying to de-ghost a ghost house."

"She feels left out, I guess. But it's strange. She went on and on about having space to herself while Caleb is at the brew festival with Aidan. So, I just thought she meant she wanted to be alone. It's like her PMS is on steroids."

"Maybe she's pregnant."

"She's not. She can't be."

"Is she barren?"

"No."

"Is she having sex with her husband?"

"Yes."

"Then it's possible." Jolie went to the fridge and grabbed a bottle of water. "I'm going to shower and then I'll be down."

"Okay," I said stupidly. I gave the veggies one last stir and then turned off the burner.

Jolie bounded out of the kitchen, her ponytail swaying and hitting her shoulders. The moment she was gone, I called Annie back.

She answered.

"Is there something you want to tell me?" I asked.

"Something like what?"

"Something like, maybe why you're acting all irrational when it has nothing to do with me."

She paused and then she said, "You know."

"Do I?"

"Yes."

"You're pregnant," I stated.

Chapter 12

"Yeah, I'm pregnant," she confirmed.

"Yay!"

"Yay," she repeated.

"Why don't you sound more excited? You got your IUD removed. That's usually a green light for little spermies to make their way up your—"

"I don't need a biology lesson," she snapped.

"I don't get it. Why are you upset if this is what you wanted? Is it because of Matilda? I know the pregnancy was hard on you, but that doesn't mean this one will be."

"It's not that," she admitted. "It's just—well, the jam business is exploding. Caleb and Aidan are kicking ass and taking names with this brew thing."

"Ah, you don't want to be forced to slow down even though you'll have to."

"Yeah," she mumbled. "You were smart to have two at a time."

"Didn't really have a choice in that regard." I paused. "Have you told Caleb yet?"

"No. I wanted to wait until he's home in a few days."

"Can you really sit on this news for that long?"

"I'd really rather do it face to face, so I'll do what I can to keep the news to myself."

"You didn't do a good job," I quipped. "I put the slightest bit of pressure on you, and you cracked like a walnut."

"Yeah, but you're you. I can't lie to you."

"What are you doing right now?" I asked her.

"Having a cup of tea and freaking out."

"You could do that down here," I said.

"Down where?"

"Gator Springs, dingus. Come down. Hang out with us. Get out of your house and your head."

"I could," she said slowly. "Caleb's mom has offered to take Matilda if Caleb and I ever want to get away together."

"Take her up on the offer," I said.

"I do need a break," she admitted.

"My beach home is your beach home. You know that, right? Like I shouldn't have even had to offer. You could've just shown up. That's what Jolie did. I've just come to expect that sort of behavior from my friends. Text me your flight time and I'll come pick you up in style."

"Okay, but can you do me a favor?"

"What?"

"Don't bring Jolie. She's lovely, don't get me wrong, but the way I'm feeling, I'm liable to snap her 5'8" twiggy body in half with my bare hands."

I chuckled. "It'll just be me. I promise."

"What are you having for dinner?" she asked.

"Pasta with veggies."

"You're feeding her carbohydrates?"

"Yup."

"And she's eating them?"

"More than that, she's the one who asked for garlic bread."

"Okay, now I know for sure something is going on with her. She's an A-list celebrity actress and they're always on weird smoothie diets."

"Let it go, Annie."

"Fine. I'll let it go. But when I see her, I'm grilling her."

"Have at her. Just leave me out of it."

She sighed. "You really are the best. You know that?"

"Nah, this is just what we do. One of us freaks out and the other is there to catch us."

"It's a good system."

"It's worked well all these years," I admitted. "See you soon."

I hung up with her and then quickly plated the food. I was just pouring two glasses of wine when Jolie strolled back into the kitchen.

"How do you do it?" I asked her as I handed her a glass of wine.

"Do what? Thanks for this, by the way." She took a sip of her wine and grimaced. "That all-in-one grocery store needs a better wine selection."

"Hmm."

"Do what?" she repeated.

"Look as fresh as a daisy," I said. "No makeup, straight out of the shower. Nothing."

"Tinted moisturizer," she said immediately.

"It's got to be more than that."

She tweaked my nose. "You're a good friend."

"Am I?"

"One of the best. I'm glad we met, Sibby. Seriously. I loved working with you in the past, and you just seem so…"

"What?"

"Grounded."

"Grounded? Me? You're not serious."

"I am serious," she said.

"Oh God," I moaned.

"What? What'd I say?"

"You called me grounded."

"So? Isn't that a good thing?"

"I don't know, maybe. Oh shit, I've gotten boring."

"You haven't gotten boring."

"You can't say that. You don't even know what I was like before."

"Before? Before what?"

"Before kids. Before marriage."

"What's marriage like?"

I grinned. "Marriage is fun. Well, it's fun if you're married to Aidan."

"Fun. Huh."

She set down her glass of wine and picked up her fork.

"You don't have fun in relationships?" I asked.

"It's been so long since I've had a normal one," she said. "A lot of Hollywood relationships are manufactured. They're just for the press."

"Seriously?"

"Yeah. The last three guys I dated were publicity stunts." She shook her head. "Sometimes I think about…"

"Think about what?"

"Pulling back," she blurted out. "It's a lot sometimes and everyone always wants a piece of you, and only because you have something they can take."

"I don't know how you do it, to be honest. Even that small blip in the public eye caused me to retreat. But people have already forgotten my face. They'll never forget yours."

"Thanks," she remarked dryly.

"Make a list," I said. "Make a list right now of the people in your life who would still be in your life if you weren't an actor and if you were flat broke."

"Do you want me to like, name them out loud?"

"Yes. You need to know who loves you for you and not because of your fame."

"See," she said. "This is what I meant about you being a good friend. Do you know that when we met, I was really nervous?"

"You were nervous? You're kidding. You were so cool."

She let out a long laugh. "You were genuine. And I hadn't been around that in a long time."

"Well, I'm glad we're buds." I took a sip of wine. "You were right."

"The wine being shit?"

"That, but also Annie. She's pregnant."

"Well, that's awesome!"

"It is." I frowned. "She's freaking out about it, so she's coming down here for a little R and R."

"That'll be nice."

"Whatever she says to you, don't take it personally."

"Whatever that means."

"It means she's hormonal and you're really skinny and hot."

"Not that skinny. Not with all the carbs and wine."

"You run like three times a day on the beach. And you start your day with Pilates and meditation. Admit it, you look great."

"Thanks." She shook her head and scooped up a bite of veggies. "You know, I've been on a diet since I was seventeen. It feels really weird to just...eat."

"Seriously? Seventeen?"

"When I was discovered." She used air quotes around the word discovered. "Hanging out with you, enjoying my free time, I realize how much I miss having control over my time and my own life."

I heard a wistful loneliness in her voice. "I'm just gonna take a stab at it and say, you're looking for something *more*. Something deeper."

She paused. "Yeah. I think I am. I've been going from project to project, and I think I just want to slow down a little."

"Kinda hard to slow down a little when you're on a hit TV show," I pointed out.

"Sibby, I—"

My phone rang. I looked down at the screen and saw a number I didn't recognize. I let it go to voicemail and turned back to Jolie. "Sorry, you were saying?"

"Never mind. Let's eat before it gets cold."

We fell silent as we enjoyed our dinner. When we finished, I said, "I'm just going to check my voicemail real quick."

"Take your time. I'll clean up."

"You sure?"

"Absolutely. You cooked. I'll do the dishes."

"This kitchen needs a dishwasher," I commented. "I've grown accustomed to luxury."

She laughed. "Modern conveniences. I never want to do without them. If someone was like, 'Your soul mate lives two hundred years in the past, will you time travel to live with him?' I'd seriously have to consider if love outweighs the advances we've made in modern plumbing."

"Love of your life versus a flushing toilet? I'll take the love of your life, please. Still," I looked around the kitchen, "I wonder if it's worth it to upgrade the kitchen, just a little bit."

"Don't get distracted. You have enough on your plate," she said.

"You're right."

"Check your voicemail, I'll clean up, then we'll tackle the photo albums and see if we can find Ray."

I saluted her and then walked out of the kitchen. I pressed my voicemail button and stuck the phone to my ear.

"Good evening, my name is Jerry Lewis and I own the Gator Springs Funeral home and Crematorium. We have Ida Adelman's ashes ready for pick up. Our hours are nine to six, Monday through Friday, ten to five on Saturday and closed on Sunday. Thank you."

The voicemail ended and I looked at my phone for a moment.

I had to pick up ashes?

I immediately called Luke. He answered on the first ring. "Hello?"

"Hi, Luke," I said. "It's Sibby."

"Hey, Sibby."

"Hey. So, I just got a call from the funeral home and Ida's ashes are ready to be picked up."

"Uh huh."

"Why didn't you tell me that I'd have to do that?"

"I'm sorry, I thought you realized that was a part of it."

"Did her will say anything about how she wanted her remains...ah, disposed of?"

"Yes, but it's completely up to you. Her will made it clear that you can do with her remains as you please."

"My choice?" I rubbed my forehead. My phone beeped. I looked at my screen. Aidan was calling me. "Sorry, that's my other line. I've got to go."

"Sure thing. Call me back if you need anything."

"Thanks." I clicked over to the other line. "Hello?"

"Is there something you want to tell me?" Aidan asked.

"Um. I love you?"

"Try again."

"I think the beach house is haunted."

He paused. "Okay, that's not what I thought you were going to say."

"What did you think I was going to say?"

"Why do you think the house is haunted?"

"There's been some ghostly trickery. I'll explain in a minute. What do you think I'm supposed to tell you that I'm not telling you?"

"Annie."

"What about her?" I hedged.

"Why is she heading down to Gator Springs to hang out with you now? She and Caleb were going to come down at the end of summer like we discussed. She's leaving Matilda with Caleb's mom."

"Wow, news travels quickly."

"She just talked to Caleb. He's flabbergasted."

"Good word choice."

"Sibby," Aidan began.

"Don't *Sibby* me. I don't know anything."

"She's your best friend."

"So? What's this about?" I asked.

"He's freaking out."

"Why?"

"Because the last time she acted all weird and squirrely she backed him in a corner, and they broke up."

"That was years ago," I pointed out. "And they've grown. Matured. She's sober. She's a mother. She's got a successful business. She moved Upstate so you and Caleb can still be business partners. We have dinner together three times a week. Do you really think she's going to do anything to jeopardize our collective relationship?"

"You *do* know something is going on," he stated. "I know you do."

"I might know something," I admitted. "But I'm sworn to secrecy."

"Is it bad news?"

"No."

"Is it good news?"

"Yes."

"Sibby!"

"Look, she's coming down here for a few days to clear her head and hang out with me. You and Caleb will be done in a few days and then you'll be down here too. They can talk then. Just tell Caleb that I've got it. Okay? When he talks to his wife face to face, he'll understand."

"What do you mean *you've got it.*"

"I mean, I'm the Annie whisperer. And sometimes you just need your best gal pal to get you through. Trust me, he *wants* me to handle this."

"We're in our thirties. Aren't we done with this keep-ing-secrets-from-each-other thing?"

"No, silly. We're basically still in high school and I don't know if the most popular boy in school likes me right now."

"I like you," he said gruffly. "I just don't like being on the outside."

"If it makes you feel any better, this has nothing to do with you. I'm keeping Annie's confidence, okay? Don't ask me to betray that."

"Best-friend clause." He sighed. "Yeah, okay. As long as you're telling me nothing is wrong."

"Nothing's wrong," I assured him. "You can tell that to Caleb. She's just trying to sort some stuff out, okay?"

"Okay. I'll tell him he has nothing to worry about."

"Good."

"Now will you tell me why you think the house is haunted?"

"I don't think, I know. Well, I don't think it's haunted anymore. We bought guardian gnomes and burned sage. We should be good now."

"Do I even want to dive further into this?"

"No, I don't think you do."

Chapter 13

I sat in bed and flipped through one of Aunt Ida's photo albums while drinking chocolate milk through a Twizzler. Jolie had gone to bed hours ago. She'd gotten discouraged when we hadn't found anything about Ray.

But the photo albums of Aunt Ida's life were astounding. They documented all her travels, all the different clothes she wore through the changing times. But what struck me most was her smile. She always had the biggest grin on her face, like she couldn't wait to gobble up every moment, every adventure.

Through her photos, I saw that she really lived. She was alone in most of the photographs. It seemed like she didn't need anyone else to have a good time.

"I wish I knew you better," I said, touching the corner of a picture, one where she's holding a huge fish toward the camera.

With a sigh, I closed the photo album and set it back in the box at the end of the bed.

I took my empty glass and headed downstairs, my mind on Ida. What had she been afraid of? Anything? It was easy to think she'd been fearless, based on her photos, but had she died with regrets? Had she yearned for a family? Or were here adventures enough?

"Sibby?"

"Gah!" I whirled, dropping the glass onto the floor.

Jolie hit the kitchen light. "Sorry, I didn't mean to scare you."

"Then don't sneak up on me in the dark."

"Why are you in the dark?" She looked around for the broom and found it tucked next to the refrigerator.

"I didn't mean to be in the dark, I was just coming down to set the glass in the sink."

"Step back," she commanded as she went for a broom and dustpan. She quickly swept up the shattered glass and dumped it into the garbage.

"I thought you went to sleep," I commented.

"I tried. I tossed and turned."

"How do you toss and turn after running on the beach, carbs, and wine?"

"You should know. I swear I can hear you pacing in your room."

I sighed. "I was thinking about Ida."

"Tea?"

"Might as well."

I sat down at the kitchen table with the laminate flowers. "Annie's flight gets in tomorrow afternoon."

"Cool. Want me to ride shot gun with you to pick her up?" Jolie took the kettle to the sink and filled it up.

"I appreciate the offer, but I think she wants me to herself for a few minutes."

"Ah, she's jealous. Got it."

"I don't know if she's jealous per se, but she's definitely feeling left out."

"Well, when you go to pick her up, I'll head to the store

and grab some fun snacks I love to eat when I'm hormonal and cranky."

"Maybe don't call her cranky when you see her," I suggested. "She already has it out for you."

"Why?"

"She's a product of emotional abandonment from her parents, therefore she has issues getting attached to people and worrying they're going to leave her. So, she's worried I'm having fun without her."

Jolie looked at me and blinked like an owl. "Is that your assessment of her? That was very psycho-analyzing."

"Nah, that was her therapist's assessment. I just repeated it. She puts up with my neurotic imposter syndrome tendencies and I put up with her abandonment issues. We're a match made in heaven."

She snorted.

"I've known her longer than I've known Aidan. Kinda wild," I said.

"Wild, indeed."

The tea kettle whistled and when Jolie went to turn off the stove, the burner blew out before she could get to it.

"Huh," she said, flipping the dial.

"That was odd."

She turned the burner back on and it immediately blew out.

"Maybe there's a draft," she said, her voice quivering.

"I don't feel a draft." A pit of anxiety balled in my stomach. "I really hope this isn't like a warning sign that the house is going to explode."

"Shit," she muttered. "It's probably a good idea to sleep somewhere else for the night."

"I'm not sleeping on the beach."

"Well, I'm not sleeping in a car."

I sighed. "I think I know someone who will let us crash."

"You sure you don't mind?" I asked.

"Nope." Luke waved us inside his home. He looked at Jolie and his jaw dropped open ever so slightly.

"This is my friend Brenda," I introduced.

"Hi," Jolie said. "Thank you so much for taking us in tonight."

Luke pulled himself together. "Seriously, it's no trouble at all."

I bit my lip to keep from grinning. Luke's cheeks were flushed, and he hastily ran a hand through his hair, but it only made him look more disheveled.

A black Scottish Terrier darted into the room, barked once, wagged its stubby tail, and then quickly zoomed away.

"That's Scottie," Luke said.

"Scottie the Scottish Terrier?" I asked in amusement.

Luke shrugged, looking embarrassed.

"Cute," Jolie flirted. "Very cute."

Luke's cheeks blazed with color. "I do have a guest room," he said, clearly changing the subject. "But I didn't mention they're bunk beds. For my nieces. I guess one of you could sleep on the pull-out couch, but it's not very comfortable."

"Bunk beds are fine," I assured him. "Thanks for not thinking we're insane."

"Weird shit happens," he said with an understanding smile.

"You weren't asleep, were you?" Jolie asked.

"No," he replied. "Can I get you something to drink? Or a snack?"

"We were just going to have tea when the, ah, incident occurred," Jolie said. "I like to enjoy a cup to unwind."

"I think I have some chamomile," Luke said. "But why don't I show you guys your room?"

We followed Luke to the spare bedroom, and he flipped on the light.

"Okay," Jolie said with a laugh. "You didn't tell us it was decorated for fairy princesses."

He rubbed the back of his neck and looked down, clearly embarrassed. "My nieces have me wrapped around their little fingers."

"You play tea party, don't you?" she teased.

"Maybe. I don't wear the tiaras, though."

"I'm not sure I believe you," she flirted.

"Let me get that water started for tea," Luke said. "Bathroom is down the hallway."

"Thanks, Luke," I said. "We really appreciate it."

"Seriously happy to do it." He looked at Jolie for a moment and then ducked out of the bedroom.

Jolie waited five seconds before closing the door. "Why didn't you tell me your lawyer was hot?"

"Uh, because I didn't think it really mattered. It doesn't affect my life."

"Do you think he knows who I am?" she asked, biting her lip.

"He didn't say anything about you looking like, well, you. He just stared at you like a love-struck teenager."

She glanced at the door.

"Go out there," I encouraged. "I'm gonna stay in here."

"Sibby, you don't have to play match maker."

"I'm not playing match maker. But you two clearly had a spark. Go explore it."

"I'm not going to ditch you."

"Ditch me," I suggested. "I'll take the top bunk."

"You sure?"

"Go for it, but I have one word of advice…"

"Yeah?" she asked.

"Tell him who you really are. He's not the type to blab. Now go. Why are you standing here talking to me when there's a cute guy trying to find out if he has chamomile tea to make you?"

"You just became a yenta, congratulations."

"Well, it was bound to happen. DNA and all that."

Jolie slipped through the door and left me alone. I hadn't bothered getting dressed and I was wearing pajamas with a unicorn pattern.

I heard the distant sound of laughter and smiled.

I thought about texting Aidan to let him know the situation but decided to call him in the morning. After I set my alarm on my phone, I shoved my cell under my pillow and fell asleep.

I woke up confused. For the last few nights, there had been a blue ceiling over my head. Now, there was a bright pink, Pepto Bismol colored ceiling.

My phone was underneath my pillow and I grabbed it. It was just past eight in the morning, and I had a missed text from Aidan.

I rolled over just enough to peer below to the lower bunk. The coverlet hadn't been disturbed, and there was no indentation on the pillow.

Did that mean…

Jolie hadn't slept in the bottom bunk!

I called Aidan, but he didn't answer, so I left a message. I made sure it didn't sound panicky or urgent, but I did want to let him know what was going on.

Moses love him, he knew my brand of crazy and rolled with it. He usually entertained it. Said it kept our marriage interesting.

I climbed down the ladder of the bunk bed and hit the floor. I hesitantly opened the door, listening for sounds of laughter or conversation…or morning hanky panky.

Either Luke had thick walls, or there was nothing going on, because I didn't hear anything.

I went to the bathroom first and tried to corral my hair.

It was no use, so I threw it up into a messy bun and then tromped into the kitchen.

Jolie was sitting at the table, eating a bagel slathered with cream cheese.

"Morning," she said, a goofy grin plastering her face.

"Morning," I said. "Where's Luke?"

"In the shower."

"Oh, really." I arched a brow. "I noticed your bed wasn't slept in last night."

"Nothing happened. I mean, we talked all night, but nothing else happened." She wiped her mouth with a napkin. "I told him who I really was."

"Did you? This just got interesting."

"He's super easy to talk to. And he's a total goof ball. He doesn't even care that I'm Jolie Kingston." She looked longingly in the direction of Luke's bedroom.

"So, you guys talked for hours and hours," I said. "What about?"

"Our families, our past relationships, favorite books and music."

"The meaning of life, then?"

"Yup. By the way, he already made a call for someone to come look at Ida's house to see about the gas leak. He's going to be there at ten."

"That was nice of him."

"It was," she said with a grin. She finished her bagel and then stood up and stretched. "I'm definitely going to need a nap before tonight."

"Tonight," I said. "You mean before Annie gets here?"

She rubbed the back of her neck. "Ah, Luke asked me to dinner. Do you mind?"

"Mind? Seriously? Hang out with me and my hormonal friend or hang out with a hot lawyer who is already smitten with you. This one is no contest."

Jolie grinned and then it slipped. "Crap. It's Friday night."

"Yeah? So?"

"So, isn't Betty Sue's book club meeting tonight?"

I groaned. "I don't want to go."

"Then call and tell her last-minute plans came up. Because they did. Annie's coming to town," she said.

"Why do I have to call her? You're the one that promised her we'd go."

"I'm sorry I spoke out of turn. Please do this for me," she begged.

"Jolie, are you *scared* of Betty Sue?"

"No, I'm not scared of her." She paused. "I'm *terrified* of her."

<hr>

Chapter 14

<hr>

"I SAW A BISON!" Sophie screeched, her face lit up with excitement. "Can I get one?"

"Where would we put it?" I asked her.

She thought for a moment. "It can stay in my room."

"They grow pretty big," I pointed out.

"Then we can get a miniature one. There are miniature ponies. There must be miniature bison."

I saw this conversation devolving quickly, so I did what I always did when I needed to get her off a topic. I said, "Let's wait and ask your father."

"I know what that means." Sophie wrinkled her nose. "You wanna talk to Ollie?"

"Yes, please."

"K, hold on." She cupped her hand at her mouth and hollered, "Ooooooooollllllllllliiiiiiieeeee."

"Thanks, Soph," I remarked dryly. "I no longer have ear drums."

A moment later, Oliver appeared on the screen. His face was smudged with dirt and his usual bowtie was missing.

"Look at you," I said with a grin. "Were you playing outside?"

He nodded.

"Ollie met a girrrrrl," Sophie teased.

"Sophie," he whined.

"Let me talk to your brother for a bit," I said to her.

"Okay. Love you. I still want a bison."

She blew me a kiss and ran off, her braids flying behind her.

"So, a girl?"

He shrugged. "Ashley likes to be outside. And I like Ashley, so…"

"How did you meet her?"

"She's at the campsite next to us. Her parents and Grandma and Grandpa started talking last night, and we had burgers and hot dogs, and chips."

"Well, I'm glad you made a friend," I said, my heart soaring. Oliver was the shy one. Sophie led and he followed. The fact that he made a friend independent of his sister was a huge win.

"Can she come to the beach at the end of the summer?" he asked.

"Ah, I'm sure she and her parents already have plans."

"But if they don't?"

"We'll see," I said, uttering the parent party line. "Love you, kiddo. Have fun."

"I will!"

He ended the call, and the screen went dark. I tossed my phone aside and pressed my head to the steering wheel of the Cadillac.

Jolie was at the house, waiting for the gas guy to arrive, and I'd driven to the funeral home to pick up Ida's ashes.

I was currently sitting in the parking lot, under a huge tree in the shade, getting up the nerve to go inside. I wasn't sure why it bothered me so much, aside from the fact that I'd never been inside a funeral home. They just seemed strange.

"I'm over thinking this," I said. "I just need to get up and go in there. It'll take ten minutes and then I'll be done."

I was just about to open the car door when my phone rang again.

"Hello, husband," I greeted.

"Hello, wife. We've been playing phone tag."

"Yup."

"What's the news from Gator Springs?" he asked.

"Jolie and I crashed with Ida's lawyer last night because of a potential gas leak, and now they're all moony eyed over each other and it's adorable."

"Gas leak?"

"Potential gas leak," I corrected.

"This lawyer…"

"Luke," I supplied.

"Right, Luke. He's really into Jolie?"

"Yeah."

"Meaning he's not in love with you."

"In love with—" A guffaw escaped my mouth. "You're not serious."

"Of course, I'm serious."

"I was wearing my unicorn pajamas," I said. "He got one look at Jolie and his jaw nearly dropped to the floor."

"You know you're attractive, right? Like, really attractive?"

"We're married. I'm a mom and a wife, and a habitual hot mess. You're my one and only. Luke has been incredible helping navigate this really weird situation, but he's not into me. I promise."

"Okay," he said, though he didn't sound like he believed me.

"Seriously? If anyone has to worry about anything, I need to worry about *you.*"

"Me? You don't have to worry about me."

"Dude, you know how I get when you wear a backwards baseball cap. I know other women feel the same way. And your dimples. My God man, your dimples…"

"Did you just *dude* me?"

"Yes."

"How do you get when I wear a backwards baseball cap?"

"I'm not gonna say it. I won't give you the satisfaction."

"Satisfaction, huh?"

"Okay, double entendre. I get it. I love you and I would never do anything to jeopardize what we have together. Furthermore, I've entered the high-waisted jeans part of life. You might find them attractive, but other males of a certain age bracket, the kind of men that want Jolie Kingston, are not interested in me or my jeans."

"I know you didn't mean it the way it sounded," Aidan said. "But I'll let it slide. You know, for a writer, you're not always the best at communication."

"I want you and no other, for now, for always, and even if you die first, I hope you come back and haunt me."

He paused. "You mean that?"

"I really do."

"Good news," Jolie said when I walked into the house carting Ida's ashes. "There's no gas leak. It's just Ray playing his wacky tricks on us."

"Lovely."

"You're in a mood."

"I almost hit a gator again."

"Another one?"

"The same one we saw."

"But you didn't hit it."

"No. I swerved."

"Then why are you so down?"

"I don't know. I just feel *off.*"

"Off?"

"Yeah, like something's brewing but I don't know what."

"Like a hurricane?"

"Like a...I don't know."

I followed her into the house and placed Aunt Ida on the mantle next to Tilly.

"I think I know the problem," Jolie said. "I'm a bit delirious from lack of sleep, so take it with a grain of salt, but I've been thinking about this house and the...issues we're facing."

"Go on," I said.

"You've got to change it."

"Change it?"

"Yeah. This was Ida's house. But it's your house now. Keeping it the way it is…maybe that's why Ray won't leave. He still thinks it's Ida's. Just speculation though. I'm not a ghost shrink or whatever."

"So, Ida's deceased lover is upset because we're here? This is insane!"

"More insane than calling your lawyer at ten at night and asking if we can crash with him because we don't know if there's a gas leak or a ghost in the house?"

The timer on my phone went off. "I've got to go pick up Annie from the airport. We can talk about this later. Have fun on your date."

I opened the front door just as a man wearing a sheriff's pin attached to his denim blue jean shirt raised his hand to knock.

"I'm looking for Jolie Kingston," he said.

I frowned and before I could reply, Jolie came to the door. "I'm Jolie. What can I do for you, Officer?"

"You're under arrest."

"*What?*" I gasped.

The sheriff looked at me. "And you're under arrest for aiding and abetting a criminal."

"I'm a criminal!" I yelled.

Jolie rolled her eyes and then leaned back against the wall of the county jail cell, like she was preparing to get truly comfortable. "You're not a criminal. You didn't do anything wrong."

"The sheriff accused me of aiding and abetting a felon," I snapped and then lowered my voice. "The car you bought at the airport was being stolen when you saw that guy!"

"It'll get sorted out. I'm not worried."

"How are you not worried? We haven't been given our one phone call, my best friend is stranded at the airport, and you're Jolie-freakin'-Kingston, and if it gets out that you—"

"It's not going to get out," she said. "How would it get out? The only person who knows my identity aside from you is Luke, and he wouldn't tell. Besides, no one even knows I'm in Gator Springs."

"What do you mean *no one knows you're in Gator Springs?* Someone must've figured it out, otherwise they wouldn't have been able to trace the stolen vehicle back to you."

"I meant my manager and everyone back in LA who

I'm connected to has no idea I'm in Gator Springs. I all but fell off the map."

"But *why?*"

"I don't want to say."

"You better say," I commanded. "I'm in the system now because of you. Do you know what this is going to do to my mother?"

"So don't tell her."

"You don't understand. Mama Goldstein has a way of knowing when I screw up. Somewhere in the space time continuum, she'll get a brain tickle, and she'll know." I buried my head in my hands. "I got put in the back of a cop car. I'm on the other side of the law!"

"You didn't do anything! This is all me. This is my fault."

"Why aren't you freaking out about it? And how did you not know you were buying a stolen vehicle?"

"It's not like the car was painted with the word STOLEN on the hood, you know?"

"It's a piece of shit! You had to know something was going on."

"I wasn't in a clear mind frame," she mumbled. "I was worried about other things."

"What other things?"

"Just…*things.*"

"Show tunes!" I yelled suddenly.

"What about show tunes?" she asked warily.

"We sing show tunes at the top of our lungs and that'll get the sheriff in here and then we can demand to make our phone call."

"I don't know any show tunes."

I stared at her in shock. "But you're a movie star."

"Yeah, so?"

"So, don't all of you guys at one point or another decide to leave Hollywood to do a Broadway musical?"

"We're not all Hugh Jackman."

I paused. "Do you know Hugh Jackman?"

"I don't see what that has to do with anything."

"Do you?"

"Yeah, I've met him. Nice fella." She raised her brows. "So, show tunes?"

"Right. What's the most annoying musical?"

"I'm not sure, but I'm inclined to say *Cats*."

"I don't know *Cats*." I paused. "Ah, got it."

I cracked my knuckles, rolled my shoulders, and then belted out, "*Go go go Joseph you know what they say!*"

"Oh God," Jolie moaned. "Someone let me out of here!"

"*Hang on now Joseph we'll make it some day!*"

"Eff my life. Eff my life and my stupid plan to come to stupid Florida to get away from my stupid life."

I paused midline and turned to look at her. "Oh my God!"

"What?" she demanded.

"My curse has finally been broken!"

"What curse?"

"The curse where I'm the one that causes all the problems and all the fires! It's *you*. Somehow my curse transferred to you. I'm free!"

I began to hop and skip around the ten by ten jail cell like Rumpelstiltskin dancing around a fire.

"I'm free! I'm free!"

The sheriff entered the room.

"That was fast," I said. "The power of Broadway showtunes..."

"Hmm. The hatred runs deep. Do we finally get to make our phone call?"

"Don't need to," he said, sticking the key in the lock. "You both made bail."

"How? Who knows we were in here?" I demanded.

"I'm guessing because it's a small town, someone saw us being taken away in a police cruiser," Jolie said, rising.

"I'm changed forever now," I commented. "I'm not who I was when we were thrown in here. I'm reformed."

Jolie rolled her eyes. "We've been in here for an hour, and nothing happened to change you."

"Speak for yourself. I'm not afraid of Ray. I can't believe you bought—"

"Don't say anything," she snapped. "Not until we have a lawyer present. I'll give mine a call when we get out of here."

I sighed. "Lawyer. Shit. We need a lawyer."

"Your lawyer's the one who bailed you out," the portly sheriff said.

"Lawyer? Oh, you mean, Luke?" I asked.

"Yep."

Jolie and I exchanged a look and then we followed the sheriff into the front area where Luke was waiting for us.

"You got a lot more than you bargained for when Aunt Ida left me her estate, didn't you?" I asked Luke.

"We haven't had this much excitement in years," he said, his gaze darting from me to Jolie. "You okay?"

She nodded, but clamped her mouth shut.

"You've made bail," the sheriff said, "but you're not free to leave the state. Not until we figure out this stolen vehicle nonsense."

"She has to be able to leave the state," I said, my tone panicky. "She has to get back to set to film the next season—"

"Sibby," Jolie interrupted. "Don't."

"Don't what?" I demanded. "You have a career. You have to get back!"

She rubbed the bridge of her nose and shot Luke a look.

"You haven't told her?" Luke asked her quietly.

Jolie shook her head. "Not yet."

"Wait, *he* knows why you're here and I don't? And also," I whirled to face the sheriff, "am I allowed to leave the state?"

"No," he said. "You're tangled up in this mess. So until it's unraveled, you're also not allowed to leave the state of Florida."

I looked at Jolie. "No offense, but I'm able to mess up my life all on my own. I don't really need your help."

Her shoulders slumped and I immediately felt terrible.

"Let's get you guys home and then you can talk," Luke said, taking Jolie's hand and giving it a squeeze.

"I can't go home," I said, taking my personal belongings from the sheriff. "I have to call Annie and find out if she's still at the airport. And now I have to call my husband and tell him what's going on and then I need to breathe into a paper bag."

I turned my phone on and it pinged with several notifications. Most of them were missed calls. Annie's texts were all shouty caps and angry face emojis. I winced and immediately called her.

"Where are you? Are you okay? Were you in an accident?" she demanded. "My plane landed forty-five minutes ago and I haven't heard from you."

"I'm sorry, I'm sorry, I'm sorry. I kinda, sorta got arrested."

She paused for a moment. "You're kidding, right?"

"No. I'm not kidding."

"How are you calling me right now—wait, am I your one phone call?"

"No. We made bail."

"We?"

"Jolie and me."

"Jolie was arrested too?"

"It was kind of her fault. Listen, I'll explain when I get there."

"I'll take a cab," she said. "You sound like you have a lot on your plate. I don't want to be a bother."

"It's not a bother," I insisted.

"Text me the address," she said. "A cab is pulling up right now."

She hung up. I immediately felt the vein in my head begin to throb.

"Everything okay?" Jolie asked.

"Fine. Annie's taking a cab from the airport."

I walked out of the building and into the sunshine.

"I'm parked around the corner," Luke said. His fingers were laced with Jolie's and she was staring at him like he was the solution to all her problems.

"Tell me now," I commanded.

"I'd really prefer not to do it out in the open," she said. "But I'll tell you the truth about why I came down here when we get back to Aunt Ida's."

I nodded.

We turned the corner of the building and Luke clicked the button to unlock his Beamer. He quickly opened the passenger side door and the rear.

I slid into the back seat and immediately buckled myself in. The car ride was silent back to Aunt Ida's house.

Ida's house. The house that brought me nothing but trouble and an arrest.

I groaned.

"What? Are you feeling okay?" Jolie asked, turning around to peer at me. "Is your blood sugar low?"

"My mood is low."

Jolie turned back around. Luke reached over and took her hand.

They were damn close for having just met the night before. But I understood insta-smitten. It had happened with me and Aidan.

I held in another groan.

Aidan. How was I supposed to tell him about this? What was he going to say? Why did nothing insane ever happen to him?

Luke pulled up to Aunt Ida's house and parked.

"Thanks, Luke." Jolie leaned over and brushed her lips against his cheek.

"Don't worry about a thing. We'll get this all sorted. The charges will be dropped before you know it," he said, smiling at her.

"How did the sheriff find out about the car being stolen?" I asked suddenly.

"It was reported stolen about a week ago," Luke said.

"Uh-huh. But how did the sheriff know the car was here?" I raised my brows. "It's not like he was trolling the neighborhood, saw the beater in front of Ida's house, and ran the plates because it looked out of place."

Jolie and I met each other's gazes.

She raised her brows.

I had a pretty good idea who tipped off the sheriff.

Chapter 15

I CLIMBED out of the Beamer and headed up the porch steps, riffling through my purse for my keys. I couldn't find them and in my complete and utter frustration, I turned over my bag and dumped its contents onto the wooden planks.

My keys were nowhere to be found. But I did have a rogue tampon that had lost its wrapper.

Seems about right.

I ran out of steam and plopped down on the top step and waited for Jolie to get out of Luke's car.

A few minutes later, Jolie came up the walkway. She turned and waved and then Luke drove away.

Jolie plunked her butt down next to me. "Why are you sitting out here? And why is your crap all over the porch?"

"Can't find my keys and I had no energy to pick up the contents of my purse and put them back where they belong."

"Oh."

She fell silent as we sat knee to knee.

"I'm sorry I got you arrested," she said finally.

"I know."

"I didn't mean to."

"I know that too."

Jolie sighed and hung her head. "I had an affair with a married costar."

"What?" I whipped my head around to stare at her.

"Yeah." She rubbed her third eye. "He said he was separated, and I've had a crush on him since forever, so I went for it. And then his wife caught us and…well, the story's gonna hit sometime in the next few days and I just wanted to be far away and hiding by the time my reputation plopped in the toilet. The producers of the show said my behavior is going to tank the likeability of my character, so they fired me."

"Oh, Jolie." I grabbed her hand and gave it a squeeze. "I'm sorry."

She shrugged. "It's my own stupid fault. I should've known better."

"Wait, your married costar? Oh, my God. You mean it was—"

"Yup."

"He's stupid hot."

"I know."

"He's fifteen years older than you!"

"I know."

"Any regrets?"

"I don't like that I was the other woman. I wish he wasn't such a shit. I wish I hadn't gotten fired from the show because the network doesn't want the bad press, but honestly? No. I don't have any regrets. Maybe that's wrong." She shrugged. "But it's how I feel."

"And I'm guessing you told Luke?"

"It just sort of…spilled out. And it was impossible to

hold it all in. He's so easy to talk to and be with. I can't believe he was the one to bail us out of jail."

"A modern-day Prince Charming."

"Seriously."

"So, they really fired you from the show?"

"Yeah. But the writers were turning my character into an idiot anyway, so I'm not that upset about it."

"And the car? Want to explain that to me?"

"Remember I told you I couldn't find a cab? Well, the truth is that I didn't want to take a cab and have the cabbie recognize me and know where I was going. I saw a guy about to drive off and I offered him cash to hand me the keys to his car. I should've realized no one in their right mind would agree to sell a car and then mail me the title later. I didn't put the puzzle pieces together until it was too late."

"You could've just used a persona with the cabbie like you're doing here."

"Yeah, well, we saw how well that worked out."

"Is it wrong that I think Betty Sue squealed?"

"That was my thought too."

"She's got busybody written all over her," I said. "Though I'm not sure what she was hoping to achieve."

"Well, to be fair, that busted Honda did look out of place here. This town is… Luke explained it to me. They all know each other. They look out for each other. They're a community. So when there's a random beat up car…I don't blame Betty Sue for calling the sheriff to run the plates. If she was even the one."

I paused for a moment and then said, "So you're not allowed to leave the state of Florida for an undefined amount of time."

"Yeah." She looked at me. "Can I still crash with you?"

"Really? You don't want to shack up with Luke?"

"I just met Luke."

"Yeah, and you guys looked like you were ready to devour each other."

She leaned her head against my shoulder. "He's a gem and doesn't deserve my mess. Plus, how would this work?"

"How would what work?"

"Eventually, the charges will be dropped. I'll go back to my life. He'll go back to his. And then what? It's not like we're dating."

"Do you want to be dating?"

"I'm a mess, remember?"

"Well from one hot mess to another, when you meet a man who is the human equivalent of a mop, ready to clean up your messes and who likes you enough to do it, you kind of do whatever you have to do to make it work."

"That doesn't sound sexy."

"It isn't sexy, and that's another secret I've revealed. *Sexy* is only part of what really matters. You know what matters the most?"

"What?"

"The moments where he runs to the store to grab you ginger ale because you're puking your guts out when you're pregnant with his kids. And those moments you realize he still loves you when he cleans up your vomit bowl or wipes snot from your feverish face when you've got the flu."

"Ew, Sibby. Ew."

"Have you ever let a guy see you when you don't look your best? Have you ever been truly vulnerable with a man?"

She sighed. "No."

"You know how you know you've found the person you're meant to share your life with?'

"How?"

"When he watches his children shoot out of your hoo-ha and then later he still wants to have sex with you. That's true love."

"They don't really *shoot* out of you, do they?"

"I did make that sound like an amusement park ride, didn't I? Labor isn't as much fun as Disneyland and funnel cake, but the reward is better."

I heard the rumbling engine of a car and a few moments later, a cab pulled up to the sidewalk and parked. The cabbie jumped out of the front seat and went to the trunk to pop it open.

The door behind the passenger seat opened and Annie climbed out. She hoisted her purse onto her shoulder and waited for the cabbie to wheel the suitcase to her.

I stood up and walked down the porch steps and went to help Annie with her luggage.

"Why does a gator cross the road?" I asked.

She blinked. "Why?"

"Because it was following a chicken."

"That wasn't funny."

I sighed. "Not even a smile."

Her lips quirked up into a tiny grin. "Hey."

"Hey."

She hugged me tightly. "You've had a day, huh?"

"Yeah, I sang show tunes and I'm a felon."

"My fault," Jolie piped up. "Not the singing of show tunes. The felon part."

Annie stared Jolie down. "Do you think this is funny?"

"No."

"You got my best friend into trouble. She can do that on her own. She doesn't need your help."

"Hey, look, I didn't mean for this to happen," Jolie said, rising.

"Okay, you two—"

They ignored me completely.

"You ran down here and immediately started causing trouble," Annie fumed.

"Sibby and I are friends. You and Sibby are friends, and you have no problem whatsoever running to her when you should be talking to your husband about being pregnant."

"Hey! How do you know I'm pregnant?" Annie glared at me. "Did you tell her?"

"I told her you were acting crazy, and she deduced the same thing I did. I confirmed it after you admitted it," I defended.

Annie looked to Jolie. "You do not get to pass judgment on my choices, my life, or what I decide to tell my husband. And Sibby and I have been friends for a long time."

"Well, you don't get to judge me for just showing up at *my* friend's house."

"That's enough," I yelled. "Both of you, go to your corners."

Jolie stuck her tongue out at Annie and then marched to the end of the porch. I took Annie's elbow and guided her to the opposite end.

"Why are the contents of your purse not in your purse?" she asked.

"Can't find my keys," I muttered.

"Oh, sure."

"Don't be mad at her," I said.

"I'm not mad at her," she said.

"Then why are you acting like a middle schooler?"

"She started it."

"Actually, you started it."

"No, *she* started it when she showed up here. You guys have been galivanting around Gator Springs having shenanigans without me."

"Are you seriously jealous that I got arrested without you?"

"Well, it's something we haven't done together…"

"We haven't gotten matching tattoos either," I pointed out.

Her blue eyes lit up with excitement.

"No," I stated. "Absolutely not."

She sighed. "Yeah, I didn't think you'd go for that. So how do we get into the house if you lost your keys?"

"There's a spare underneath the alligator statue," I said.

"Speaking of alligators, we almost hit one on our way here," Annie said.

"You too?" I asked. "I've nearly hit the same gator twice. Big white stripe down its back."

"That was the one we almost hit!" she exclaimed. Annie's cell phone rang and she dug through her purse to extract it. "It's Caleb." She pressed a button and put the phone to her ear. "Hey. Yeah, I made it."

Annie stepped off the porch and walked a few feet away for some measure of privacy.

"How are you going to drive the Cadillac if your keys are missing?" Jolie asked.

"One problem at a time, please. I beg you."

"Sorry. Listen, why don't we have a bonfire on the beach and bury the hatchet tonight…before Annie buries one in my back."

"She won't do that. And if she tries, I'll stop her," I remarked dryly.

"Thanks."

"So, I kind of did a thing," Annie said as she trekked back toward the house.

"What kind of thing?" I asked. "You told your husband you're pregnant?"

"No. I kind of accidentally told him you'd gotten arrested."

"Annie!" I snapped. "What the hell?"

"I'm sorry! It sort of slipped out. He asked about my flight and then I told him about almost hitting the gator and he assumed that meant *you* almost hit the gator and I said it was the cab driver. Then he asked why I was in a cab and—"

I groaned. "Noooooooooo."

"Then I had to explain why I had to take a forty-five-minute cab ride to Gator Springs. And I didn't have a good lie ready so it just kind of slipped out."

"Now your husband is going to tell my husband and—"

My phone started to ring.

"Well, this'll be fun," I muttered. I answered my cell. "Hello?"

"Hello? That's all you've got to say to me?" Aidan asked.

"Caleb told you, didn't he?"

"Told me what?"

"That I did a stint in the pokey because I got arrested with Jolie."

"What were you doing?" he asked. "Is this like the time with the *Manischewitz* wine coolers and your public urination citation?"

"I did that *once*. Why won't you let me forget it?"

"I had to hold your purse for you," he said dryly. "I'm an enabler. It's bad. So, what happened?"

I quickly explained about the stolen car.

"So you weren't directly responsible." He sighed. "Jesus, you had me worried. Who bailed you out of jail?"

"Luke."

"Luke?"

"Yeah. I can't leave the state until this is sorted out." I paused. "You're not laughing."

"Nope."

"You usually laugh at my antics."

"This isn't an antic. This involves the law."

"It's not my fault! And please, whatever you do, don't tell my mother." I sighed. "Are you mad?"

"No."

"Surprised?"

"Really? With you I've come to expect anything."

"You sound disappointed, which is worse than being mad."

"Ahhhhhhhhh!" Jolie screamed.

I whirled around, the phone still to my ear. "What the hell is wrong with you?"

"Me?" Aidan asked.

"Not you. Jolie. Didn't you hear that shriek?"

I looked in the direction where Jolie was pointing. The gator with the white stripe was waddling down the street in front of the house. It turned its long reptilian snout toward me. We locked eyes.

"I don't do nature!" I yelled.

"It's coming for us!" Annie shouted.

"Aidan, I've got to go." I hung up on my husband before he could protest, and I shoved my cell in the back pocket of my jeans. "Into the house!"

"Where's the key?" Jolie asked.

"It's under the statue," I said.

"Go get it," Annie commanded.

"You go get it!" I snapped. "The gator is coming and I don't know how fast they run."

"Roof," Jolie stated. "We need to get up onto the roof."

"How?" Annie demanded. "The trellis won't hold our weight."

"That gator is booking it," I noted as the gator scrabbled out of the street and onto the sidewalk. "We better come up with a plan soon!"

Jolie hoisted herself up onto the plank railing of the porch and reached for the metal pipe installed onto the side of the house. She shimmied up the pipe and disappeared.

"Did she just *Cirque du Soleil* that?" Annie asked.

"Yeah, I think she did," I said.

"Should we follow her?" Annie wondered.

"No. You're pregnant and I'm accident prone."

I heard Jolie grunt and then curse, followed by the sound of sticky wood unsticking. "I'll be right down!"

A few moments later, the front door opened.

We didn't have a moment to spare.

The gator was climbing up the stairs of the porch. With a screech, I grabbed Annie's suitcase and hauled it inside. I got Annie into the foyer, quickly darted in after her, and then slammed the door shut.

"He—ah—kinda got into your purse," Jolie said as she peered through the front window. "What do you have in there?"

"Aside from a wrapper-less tampon? I have a tin of strawberry lip balm, a packet of Goldfish crackers, a box of Band-Aids, cyanide. The usual things."

"Cyanide?" Jolie repeated.

"She's kidding," Annie said.

I looked out the window and watched the gator take my purse in its large jaws and toddle away, but only as far as the front lawn, where it made itself at home and ripped the leather to shreds.

"That was my favorite bag," I said with a sigh.

Chapter 16

"I THINK you've just become an official member of the Hot Mess Express clean-up crew," I said to Luke, handing him an alcoholic beverage.

The gator was gone, taken away by animal control. I'd been informed that the gator was actually Burt, the mascot of Gator Springs. Everyone in town had thought Burt died because he hadn't been seen in three years.

Apparently, I was the Pied Piper of gators.

"Gator Springs was due for some scandal," Luke commented. "You've brought a lot of entertainment."

We sat on the front porch swing. I was covered in bug spray, but the mosquitoes didn't care. They gnawed at me like Burt had gnawed the straps of my leather bag. The bag was ruined, but my wallet was still intact, oddly enough.

Annie was laying down in a guest room—not the china doll room. Jolie was on the phone with someone in LA. Her manager or PR agent, I wasn't sure which.

Luke had swung by to return my keys. They'd fallen

out of my bag and had been on the floor of the back seat of his Beamer. I'd asked him to stay.

"So, your friend came to town?" Luke asked, sipping on his lemonade and vodka.

"Annie, yeah. Our husbands are coming down in a few days to join us. Aidan's not…"

"Aidan's not what?" he prodded.

"Happy that I got arrested."

"Did you explain the circumstances?"

"Of course. But you have to understand. I'm kinda known for this stuff."

"Getting arrested?"

I snorted. "Not specifically. Causing trouble. Disasters just kind of follow me. If the next hurricane hits Gator Springs while I'm in town, you know it was me."

"Not the fact that it's hurricane season?"

"Nope. The next hurricane will be named Sibby, I guarantee it."

"We're on the letter M."

"I don't make the rules, but the storm's coming, I promise."

"So now you manipulate the weather?"

"Yes."

"Fascinating."

I took a sip of my own beverage. "Why are you being so nice to me?"

"Aside from the fact that I'm your lawyer?"

"Yeah."

"You're under the age of forty."

"So we're friends by default?"

"Well, I just seem to have more in common with you than I do with Norm or Ralph. They like to talk about colon issues and medications, and I don't have anything to contribute to that topic of conversation."

I grinned. "I see why Jolie likes you."

"She likes me?" He beamed.

"She likes you," I assured him.

"Did she finally tell you? About why she's here?"

"She did, yeah."

He nodded and drank a long swallow of his drink.

"Does it bother you? Her past, I mean?" I asked him.

"No."

"No?"

"I've got a history, too, you know. A sordid history. I dated all the ladies and broke all their hearts…"

I stared at him for a moment. "You're a serial monogamist, aren't you?"

"Yep. How'd you guess?"

"Just followed my nose on that one."

"You really shouldn't be worried about this arrest. I've known Sheriff Lamont for a while. He's a good guy. I can call your husband and tell him if you want."

"I don't think that would help," I said, not wanting to admit that Aidan was putting off strange jealousy vibes. "I'm not worried. I mean, not really. It'll get sorted. Jolie could use some cheering up, though. She's kind of at a crossroads in life, you know?"

I fell silent and stared up at the planks of the porch ceiling.

"I was going to ask if she wanted to walk on the beach with me," he said.

"That's romantic."

"It is, isn't it?"

"I'll get her," I said. I got up from the porch swing and went into the house. It was quiet as I went up the stairs to the second floor and knocked on Jolie's bedroom door.

There was no answer.

I knocked again.

"Come in," came her muffled reply.

I went into her room. She was a lump underneath the covers of the bed.

"Luke wants to take you for a romantic walk along the beach."

"I'm tired."

"And hiding."

"And hiding," she agreed.

She popped her head out from underneath the blanket. "I just got off the phone with my publicist."

"And?"

"And the story of me and my costar is going to hit the tabloids tomorrow."

"So, you're preemptively preparing for the onslaught?"

"Yeah."

"Go for a walk with Luke. It'll make you feel better."

"Don't wanna."

"Can you change the story?"

"No."

"Can you change if it comes out or not?"

"No."

"Then pretend like it doesn't exist. That's the other Jolie. The celebrity Jolie. Go be the normal Jolie who isn't famous and just likes a boy and gets to hold his hand and dream about the future like a normal person."

She sat up. "How do I look?"

"Vulnerable, beautiful, and in need of a strong Luke shoulder to cry on. If you're nice to him, he might share his vodka lemonade with you."

There was suddenly the sound of two men talking downstairs.

I frowned. "What the hell?" I bounded off Jolie's bed. Just as I entered the hallway, Annie opened the door to her room and stuck her head out.

"What's going on?" she asked.

"No idea," I said. "I was going to investigate."

The three of us traipsed down the stairs and out onto the porch. My mouth gaped open.

"What are you doing here?" I demanded.

Aidan looked at me, a glare splashed across his face. "Hello to you too."

"I just mean—you didn't tell me you were coming!"

"It was a surprise," he said, glancing at Luke who straightened his spine. "So, surprise."

"Surprise," I murmured. "Aidan have you met Luke? Luke is my—and Jolie's—lawyer."

"We've met," Luke said. His gaze slid to Jolie. "Do you want to take a walk on the beach?"

"Yes," she squeaked. "Let's go! Aidan, it's good to see you."

"Good to see you too, Jolie," Aidan said.

"Sorry I got your wife in trouble! Luke will get her out of it, I promise!"

Jolie and Luke linked hands and passed Aidan as they walked down the porch steps.

"I smell the testosterone in the air," Annie stage whispered.

"Where's Caleb?" I asked.

"Flying down with Matilda tomorrow," Aidan answered, with a look directed at Annie.

I glanced at Annie over my shoulder. "Did you know about that?"

"I might have," she said.

"And did you know Aidan was flying down to surprise me?"

"Oh look, I have to go inside and wash my hair. Bye!"

Annie shut the front door, and I looked at my husband.

"You're wearing a backwards baseball hat," I said.

"Yup."

"You're so hot."

"Yup." A sudden grin flashed across his face. "Are you going to show me how glad you are to see me?"

I ran to him and jumped into his arms. "I can't believe you're here." I buried my nose in his neck.

"Why?"

"Because the brew festival."

"You needed me more than the brew festival needed me."

I sighed.

"Why didn't you ask me to come?" he asked.

"Because I—I don't know. I just, we had Luke. We were handling it."

"Luke," he gritted out.

"Easy tiger. Didn't you see the way he looked at Jolie before they took off? You've got nothing to worry about."

He changed the subject. "Are you sure he's capable of getting the charges dropped?"

"You have a better idea of how to handle it than having an attorney do it?"

"Calling your parents and getting your father's recommendation on a lawyer might be good."

"No. Absolutely not."

"What's Jolie saying about all this? She can't be stuck here. She has to get back to her life."

I sighed. "Sit down. There are some things I should tell you."

"Sibby," Aidan whispered.

"Hmm?"

"Sibby, wake up."

I yawned, my mouth stretching wide. "I'm so comfortable, don't make me move."

"You have to move because I have to go to the bathroom," he said. "And you're wrapped around me like an anaconda."

With a groan, I disentangled myself from my husband and rolled over. He switched on the lamp on the bedside table and sat up, giving me a lovely view of his back.

When he came back to bed, I was at a diagonal, hugging his pillow.

"Gonna make some room for me?" he asked with a grin.

"Fight me for it."

"I will. This bed is surprisingly comfortable."

We wrestled for a moment and then I reluctantly moved back to my side of the bed so he could slide under the covers.

"You were right about this house," he said.

"It's haunted?"

He laughed. "No. It's dope."

"Dope?"

"Lit," he said.

I laughed. "You and your old man slang."

"What can I say, I'm a dad. I have to become uncool."

"Never gonna happen. You're Aidan Kincaid. You will always be cool."

"Yeah, to you, maybe."

I snuggled against him.

"The kids are going to love it here."

"I miss them. I missed you too. I'm glad you're here."

"Yeah? I'm not ruining your girls' only fort?"

"Nah. Jolie is smitten with Luke," I said. "And Caleb's going to be here tomorrow anyway, right?"

"Yep."

"Let's go out to dinner tomorrow night and let Annie and Caleb have some time together."

"What do you know that I don't?"

"I can't tell you. We've been over this."

"What if I guess? Twenty questions?"

I thought for a moment. "Okay, that sounds fair. Then I'm not really breaking the best friend clause if you nail it."

"She's pregnant."

I gasped. "How did you know?"

"I didn't. Not until you confirmed it."

"You rat! You tricked me!"

"Can I let you in on a secret?" he asked.

"If you must."

"I already had an idea that might be the case."

"How?"

"She was texting Caleb every five seconds while we were at the brew festival. It was very out of character. She's not normally so…"

"Needy?"

"Yeah."

I scratched the back of my neck. "So, does Caleb know?"

"He wasn't completely sure, but yeah, he had an idea."

"Is that why he let her come down here without busting her chops over it?"

"Yup."

"Is he excited?"

"Ecstatic." He frowned. "I don't get it, though. Why is Annie freaking out? They wanted another one."

"You know when you have your life exactly the way you want it?"

"Uh, no. Every time we have our lives exactly the way we want them, Sophie shoves something up her nose and winds up in the ER or you inherit a haunted house—"

"Or you and Caleb start another business and disappear for weeks on end."

"That's my point. Life is rarely calm or routine."

"I guess she likes her life the way she likes it. And even though they wanted another, that was in theory. Now it's a reality."

"They'll figure it out." Aidan's stomach rumbled. "You never did feed me before you had your way with me."

"I can feed you now if you want. And tomorrow morning, I'll take you for breakfast at Bob's."

"The raccoon bar?"

"It's more than just—you know what? Just wait. I won't do it justice if I try to describe it."

Chapter 17

I TOSSED Annie the keys to the Cadillac. "There's a polka dot scarf in the glove box for your hair. Have fun, and call if you're going to be out past curfew."

"Thanks," she said, gripping the keys. She looked forlornly at my cup of coffee.

"You can always have decaf," I said with a winsome smile.

"What's the point," she muttered.

"He's going to be happy."

"I know."

"Are you happy?"

"When I'm not panicking about how this is going to change everything again, I'm ecstatic. Where's Aidan?"

"Still sleeping. I think those early mornings and late nights at the brew festival finally caught up with him."

"Ah."

The front door opened, and Jolie blew in like a hurricane. For the first time since I'd known her, she finally looked...*human*. Disheveled hair, blood shot eyes, nary a trace of lip gloss or mascara.

"Whoa, wild demon alert," I said.

"Jolie, do you want coffee?" Annie asked.

"I want to dig a hole on the beach and then jump inside and let the ocean swallow me."

Annie raised a brow. "So that's a solid *no* on the coffee, then?"

"The story hit, didn't it?" I asked.

"Yup," she confirmed glumly.

"About you and your co-star?" Annie asked.

She nodded. "But that's not all. Sibby is in the tabloids too…"

"*Me?*" I asked. "How am I in the tabloids?"

"Well, somehow my location got leaked and there are photos…"

"Photos of what?"

"Photos of us coming out of the county jail."

"No," I whispered.

Jolie winced. "Yeah."

There was a knock on the front door.

I buried my head in my hands. "Why do I feel like I'm living in a French farce?"

"In a French farce, people would just walk into your house without knocking," Annie said. "I'll get the door."

"I'm sorry, Sibby," Jolie said.

"It is what it is," I replied. "This isn't my first rodeo with public shenanigans."

"How can you be so calm about this?" she demanded.

"The same way you were calm about us getting arrested."

Annie returned to the kitchen with Betty Sue trailing behind her.

Great.

"Good morning, Sibby," Betty Sue said. "Brenda. Or should I say Jolie?"

"It *was* you!" Jolie shouted, pointing a finger at Betty Sue.

"Me what?" Betty Sue asked innocently.

"You're the reason Sibby and I were arrested!"

"I'm not the reason," Betty Sue said, puffing out her chest. "*You* were the reason you were arrested. It's not my fault you bought a stolen car."

"No. I take responsibility for that," Jolie said. "But I think you might've been the one to tip off the sheriff and have him check the plates."

"You were going by the name Brenda," Betty Sue said, frustration evident in her tone. "I knew you weren't who you said you were, and I was right!"

"As much fun as this is," Annie interjected, "I have to get going."

"Drive safe," I said.

"I will." Annie darted out of the kitchen and a moment later, the front door opened then closed.

"Okay, you," I pointed at Jolie. "Sit over there. And Betty Sue, you sit there. We're going to get everything out in the open."

Betty Sue crossed her arms over her chest and looked away.

Jolie wrinkled her nose at me, but reluctantly plopped her bottom down in the chair.

Betty Sue inhaled sharply and stared over my shoulder.

I turned. Aidan was sauntering into the kitchen, dressed in a pair of gray sweats and a white T-shirt.

He stopped when he realized there were three pairs of eyes watching him.

"That's how he looks first thing in the morning?" Jolie asked.

I nodded.

"Damn," she murmured.

"I know," I said with a wry grin.

"Morning," Aidan said, his eyes sleepy and dreamy. He went to the coffee maker and poured himself a cup.

"Aidan, this is Betty Sue."

"Nice to meet you," he said, coming over and holding out his hand. "Sorry you're seeing me like this. I just woke up."

"It's fine," she squeaked, her manicured hand taking his and giving it a hearty shake.

I met his gaze and decidedly not discreetly gestured for him to leave.

"I'm just gonna go…somewhere else," Aidan quipped. "Nice to meet you, Betty Sue."

"Same," she called after him.

"Okay," I said when he was gone. "My tolerance is pretty low right now. I've got a lot on my plate, and I'm not getting roped into juvenile high school crap. Betty Sue."

"Hmm?"

"I'm not selling the house," I said firmly. I met her gaze. "I've heard from other people in Gator Springs that you've wanted my Aunt Ida's house for a long time so you can turn it into a bed and breakfast. I'm very sorry, but I'm keeping the house. I hope you understand my decision."

"Does that mean—are you staying, then?" Betty Sue asked.

"For the time being. I'm going to become a part of Gator Springs. Me and my family. I hope you were sincere when you brought me food and offered to help in any way you could."

Her expression softened. "I did mean it. But I won't lie and say I wasn't going to make you an offer on the house."

"I appreciate your honesty."

Betty Sue looked at Jolie. "I really didn't mean to cause you trouble. I'm just—protective of this town, and something about the car didn't sit right. I didn't mean to drag your reputation through the mud."

"Don't worry about it," Jolie said. "I did that all on my own."

My phone rang and I fished it out of my pocket. "It's my mother."

Had she heard about the criminal charges? Had she seen the tabloids? Avoiding her wouldn't do any good.

I answered the call. "Hey, Mom. How's it going?"

"Oh, fine." She fell silent.

"What's going on, Ma?" I asked with a sigh.

"You're my daughter and I love you. But you don't photograph very well when you're coming out of a county jail."

I winced. "You saw the photos."

"Yes, I saw the photos. And you know where and when I saw the photos? I was at the Women's Lunch at the Temple, and Cheryl Applebaum sashayed up to me and she was positively gloating. She couldn't wait to tell me what she saw online."

I groaned.

"I'm your mother. I need to know about these things."

"These things? Like you want a head's up that I'm in the tabloids with false charges?"

"Yes, exactly! I need to be able to defend you without looking like I have no idea what I'm talking about, because I didn't have any idea what I was talking about. You're lucky I have a strong heart."

"I didn't do what they accused me of doing."

"Of course you didn't. I'm the captain of Team Sibby, you know that. Anyway, that dirty rotten scoundrel Cheryl... Did I tell you she got her lips done?"

I snorted. "No."

"Well, she did. And they look amazing."

Ah, the real source of my mother's anger. Not me, Sibby the Screw Up. But her rival at Temple Shalom.

Well, at least the heat was off me.

"Your father wants to speak to you," Mom said. "I'm handing you over to him."

I winced, even though Dad couldn't see me. I was already preparing for the *I'm disappointed in you* speech. No matter how old I got, whenever I disappointed my parents, I felt like a failure.

"Hi, Wapa," he said.

"Hi, Dad."

"You should've called me immediately," he said. "I can always get you a good lawyer."

"I have a lawyer."

"Who?"

"Luke Merrill. He's the one handling Aunt Ida's estate."

"Then he's not a criminal attorney?"

"I'm not a criminal."

"According to the state of Florida you are. Sibby, this is serious."

"I know, Dad. I know. Jolie's called the big guns in LA. She's got a team to sort out this mess and this is a small town. Luke knows the sherriff on a first name basis. Just... let it all play out, okay?"

"We're coming down there."

"What?"

"We're coming down. We're not waiting until the end of the summer. We'll see you in a few days. You need us. And if I see any paparazzi lurking in bushes, I'm gonna—"

"You're gonna what?" I asked, unable to contain my smile.

"I'm gonna take the camera and...and... probably just scratch the lens because I really don't like fighting."

"You're a better father than Ward Cleaver."

"High praise. Ward Cleaver was the best father of his TV generation. I stand by that."

"Thanks, Dad," I said softly. "Thanks for coming."

"Any time, kiddo. Anytime."

"Dad?"

"Yeah."

"Are you mad at me?"

"Mad? Not even a little."

"What about upset? Are you upset that I've found myself in yet another hot mess?"

"Ah, Sibby. You're nothing if not predictable. All aboard the hot mess express! Choo Choo!"

A low chuckle escaped my lips. "I would pretend to be offended, but who are we kidding?"

"Never lose your sense of humor."

"I won't. Are you guys flying or driving?"

"We'll drive. We want our own car. We'll leave early tomorrow morning."

"I'll make sure the doll room is clear."

"Doll room?"

"Yeah. We've got kind of a full house at the moment. Annie just went to the airport to pick up Caleb. Jolie is still here. I'll clean out the china doll room for you and Mom."

"I never did like dolls."

If Chucky divorced his bride and then started to date, he could harem it up with Ida's doll collection.

"Love you, Dad."

"Love you, Wapa."

I hung up with my father and let out a sigh of relief.

Jolie strode out of the kitchen and said, "I couldn't help but listen...because I was trying to."

I sniggered. "And?"

"And I'll find some other place to stay."

"What are you even talking about? There's plenty of room."

"Yeah, I know, but I don't want to intrude now that your family will be down here."

"The Goldstein clan will want to protect you too, Jolie. That's what they do."

Betty Sue appeared in the kitchen doorway and then came down the hallway into the foyer. I'd forgotten she was even here.

"Oh," I said. "I'm sorry. I didn't mean for that to take so long."

"That's really okay," she said. "I'm the one that barged in on you. So, your parents are coming to town?"

"You heard that, too, huh?"

"Yes. Will you let me host a party for them? I just love parties!"

"Why would you want to do that?" I asked, still feeling suspicious of her. I was a New Yorker through and through. Whenever someone was nice to me, I expected them to ask me for a favor. Or a cigarette.

"I'd like a clean slate," she said. "I'm afraid I've made a bad impression, and I'd really like to meet your family. Since you're planning on keeping the house, I think it would be nice to welcome you officially to the community."

I took the olive branch for what it was. "Thanks, Betty Sue. That's very nice of you and I'm happy to accept it."

"And I'll help you clean out the china doll room even though they terrify me," Jolie said. "It's the least I can do after all the trouble I've caused."

"The dolls don't stand a chance against us. There's safety in numbers," I quipped.

"How about a party in a few days? Give your parents

some time to settle in and let all this dust settle?" Betty Sue asked.

"That sounds great. Thanks."

I impulsively hugged her and then waved goodbye as she left.

The moment she was gone, Aidan reappeared, looking a little bit more alert. His hair was still a mess.

"What?" he asked when I stared at him.

"You're cute."

He rolled his eyes, but smiled, his dimples popping out front and center.

"And that's my cue," Jolie said. She skipped upstairs.

"My parents will be here tomorrow," I said to Aidan. "Mom saw the photos and she and Dad want to come down and lend their moral support. It's going to be a full house."

Aidan rubbed his scruffy jaw. "I just spoke to my parents."

"Oh no. They saw the tabloids too, didn't they? They're not rejecting me as their daughter-in-law, are they?"

"Their call had nothing to do with you, actually." He grinned. "Their travels have gone a bit awry."

"What happened?"

"Sophie happened."

"Uh-oh. What did she do?"

"She wanted to help Grandpa empty the RV tanks. She yanked one of the handles too hard and it broke. They dropped the RV off for repair and checked into a hotel for a few days while it gets fixed."

"She really is my daughter."

"Oliver informed me they're having dinner at the Meat Palace."

"The Meat Palace?"

"It's like an off-brand Texas Roadhouse."

"I see."

"Listen, I'm really hungry. Should we cook?"

"No. God, no. We'll go to Bob's. I was supposed to take you last night, but we got a bit distracted." I smiled at him. "By the way, I think Ray has gone to the other side. I haven't heard from him in a while. The guardian gnomes and smudging must've worked."

"I need more coffee."

Chapter 18

"THAT WAS the most ridiculous place I've ever eaten at," Aidan said. "It was like a rogue Margaritaville circa 1997."

"But the food was outstanding, wasn't it?"

"It was."

"Norm liked you."

"That's because I told him I'd go swamp rat hunting with him. I don't think he expected me to say yes."

"You did surprise him."

I unlocked the front door and went inside. The house was quiet. Jolie was probably out for a run or with Luke, pretending she wasn't completely into him.

"Listen," I whispered to Aidan.

"What am I listening for?" Aidan whispered back.

"There's no one here." I smiled. "You know what that means?"

He reached for me. "I know what that means…"

"A quiet moment to sit in the living room," I said, as I took his hand.

"Yeah, that's not what I was expecting."

"I have a full belly. Kind of hard to get rowdy."

"Hey, what was the meat in the dish Norm served?"

"Better if you don't ask."

We plopped down onto the couch and I leaned against him, getting comfortable. "This is nice."

"Very nice," he agreed, his hand stroking my hair.

The front door opened.

"Relaxation-interruptus," I quipped.

"Sibby? Aidan?" Annie called out.

"In the living room," I shouted back.

"Go find Sibby," Caleb said.

A few moments later, Matilda ran into the living room and draped herself across my knees and then gave me a cheesy grin.

"You're here!" I said, scooping her up into my arms.

She buried herself against me for just a moment and then launched herself at Aidan.

Caleb and Annie entered the living room, both looking happy and lovesick.

I arched a brow at Annie who cleared her throat. "We have news."

"Do tell," I said smugly.

Annie glanced at Caleb who wrapped his arm around his wife. He stared deep into her eyes and said, "They already know, don't they?"

"Yup." Annie smiled.

Aidan stood up and settled Matilda over his shoulder like a sack of potatoes. She squealed in excitement, even as she wiggled to get down.

"Congratulations," Aidan said, embracing Annie with one arm and then shaking Caleb's hand.

I got up and went to my best friend. "You guys are good?"

She sighed. "Very good. I don't know why I always worry. Things work out. Every time."

"I'm hungry!" Matilda shrieked.

Aidan plopped Matilda into Caleb's arms. "She's all yours."

"I've never been friends with a felon before," Caleb teased. "Am I a badass by association?"

"You're not even a little bit of a bad ass," I ribbed. "Because I'm in no way shape or form a bad ass. This is an extreme case of *whoops*. It'll get sorted out. Hopefully soon."

"Right. The whole not being able to leave the state of Florida thing." Caleb grinned. "Freakin' hilarious."

"Tell that to my parents," I said. "They're coming down for moral support." I used air quotes for *moral support*. "But I'm pretty sure it's so my mother can lecture me in person while also trying to tame the frizz." I gestured to my messy top bun that resembled a squirrel's nest.

"I'm always amazed by the drama in your life," Annie said. "It's like going to the theater, a one woman show titled, 'What will she get into next?'"

"You're so not being sensitive," I said.

"I'd be sensitive if I thought you were truly upset about it," she said. "But drama follows you."

"We should tell them about Sophie," Aidan said, as we all went into the kitchen.

"Nice change of subject," Caleb said. "I was afraid the two of them were going to rumble."

"Oh please, we haven't rumbled in years," Annie said. "So, what about Sophie?"

"My super villain powers are genetic," I announced. "Though I think it only affects the females of my blood-line. Oliver seems to have been spared."

"What did Sophie do?" Annie asked as she found a pot and filled it with water.

"She broke the RV poop tank handle," Aidan said.

Caleb blinked as he jangled Matilda on his hip. "You're kidding."

"Nope."

"It comes in threes, you know," Annie said. "Sibby got arrested, Sophie broke the poop tank, and there's got to be one more thing that happens."

"Don't say that." I groaned. "Now something bad is bound to happen."

I looked up from my computer screen to find Jolie standing over me. "Gah! How long have you been there?"

"About thirty seconds. Man, you get in the zone."

"I wasn't in the zone. I was watching cat videos on the internet."

"That still takes deep concentration."

"What's up?"

"Luke asked me to crash with him. And I'm going to take him up on the offer."

"Well, well, well, aren't you two smitten kittens."

"He's real," she said. "Like no bullshit. I really need that in my life right now."

"I get it. Believe me, I get it. You won't be a stranger, will you?"

"Not even a little bit. I'll walk right in like I own the place."

"Please do." I smiled. "And have fun with Luke. Does that mean you guys are going to show up at Betty Sue's party together?"

She smiled. "I think we just might."

"You sure that's a good idea?"

"Why? Because it looks like I'm jumping into a relationship while my reputation is in the toilet?"

"No. I'm thinking about what this will do to Luke if the paparazzi get wind of your budding relationship. You're Jolie Kingston and you've always been in the limelight."

"We talked about it, actually."

"Already? My, my, you guys do move fast."

"Slow down and you might miss something."

"That's very Ferris Bueller of you."

"Sometimes your life has to turn into an epic dumpster fire to illuminate what's truly important. I'm pretty sure Plato said that, but don't quote me on it."

"I'll verify it before I get it tattooed on my body," I joked. "Well, as long as you're happy."

"You know what? I kind of am."

"I'm glad to hear that."

She gestured to my computer. "I'll let you get back to your cat videos."

When the house was silent once again, I closed the cat video window and opened a blank document. This thing with Ida and Ray had my imagination whirling.

I started to type some bullet points and immediately got the spinning wheel of death. A few seconds later, it disappeared. I began to type again and then hit the space bar. It felt sticky. I tapped it a few more times and then a shock zapped my finger.

"Ow!"

A few seconds later, the computer screen flashed like it was having an acid trip flash back and then it fritzed one last time, going dark.

"No," I whispered.

I tapped the space bar.

Nothing.

I pressed the power button.

Nothing.

Well, at least I didn't set it on fire—

Sparks shot out from the wall outlet where my computer charger was plugged in.

"Ahhh!" I yelled, instinctively leaning back in my chair. The chair tipped over and I fell to the floor. "Owwwwww!"

The sparks were still snapping and popping as I scrambled up. I looked around the kitchen, my eyes locking on the fire extinguisher. I rushed for it, got my hands around it, and pulled the pin. I aimed the nozzle at the wall outlet and let it rip. Powder went everywhere.

Everywhere.

Once I was sure the sparks were subdued, I grabbed the charger and yanked it from the wall. Unfortunately, I skidded along the floor and went down.

Again.

Aidan rushed into the room and helped me stand, hugging me to him. "What happened?"

"Guess."

"You and technology?"

"Yup. I broke a laptop."

"How? It was brand new."

"I have no idea. You know I have no clue about how my powers work."

The back door opened, and Annie and Caleb

came in. Annie had a sleepy Matilda against her shoulder. They both looked at the destruction in the kitchen.

"What the—" Caleb began.

"Don't," I begged. "Just help me clean up, okay?"

"I just don't get it," Aidan said.

I held out my palm. "I'll take that five bucks now."

"We didn't bet any money," he said.

"But I did say I didn't think there was an electrical issue and the electrician confirmed that nothing is wrong with the wiring in the house."

"It just doesn't make sense," he muttered.

Annie came into the kitchen, still wearing her beach attire. "So? What did the electrician have to say?"

"That the house is fine. He checked the breakers, and the hot water heater is back on."

"Excellent. Then I can take a shower." She walked to the fridge and pulled out a bottle of water. "What are we doing for dinner?"

"Bob's?" I asked.

"We just ate there," Aidan said. "We could cook."

"And by *we*, you mean…" I raised my brows.

"Don't look at me," Annie said. "I'm exhausted. I was hoping for a pizza or something."

"There's no pizza place in this town."

"I'm salivating for a thin crust," Annie moaned.

"And pepperoni," I added.

Aidan rubbed his jaw. "And mushrooms."

"No mushrooms," Caleb said as he entered the kitchen.

"You don't even know what we're talking about," Annie said with a laugh.

"I heard pepperoni, so I assumed that meant pizza. It sounds good. Let's order," Caleb said as he walked to the fridge.

"That's what we're discussing," Aidan said. "There is no pizza place in town."

Caleb's eyes widened. "You're kidding."

"Nope. I never kid about pizza," Aidan said.

Caleb grabbed a beer and held it out to me. I shook my head. He handed it to Aidan. "This town has shit for beer, too."

"No pizza, no beer," I muttered. "It's like a modern Greek tragedy. Man, someone could make a killing opening up a brick oven pizza and beer place."

The kitchen fell silent, and my gaze darted from Aidan to Caleb and then to Annie. Aidan's brow was already furrowed, like he was formulating a business plan on the fly. Caleb looked at the beer in his hand, like he was imagining his own label on it.

"We've got the beer sorted," Aidan said slowly. "But we'd need Annie's expertise for the pizza…"

"Oh my God," she said. "You guys haven't even talked about it yet and you're already formulating a business plan. Are you serious?"

"It would be kind of cool," Caleb said. "The only shop in town."

"But how would we even—I mean, I'm—and Matilda—"

"We make it seasonal," Aidan interrupted. "In New England, there are tons of places that are open seasonally. Why can't we do that here? We can spend winters down here, see how things go. Eventually, we open during summer."

"I like that plan," I said.

"I support it," Caleb added.

"Wait, wait, wait," Annie said. "You guys are jumping ahead. What do we do about the children?"

"Bring them with us, obviously," I said.

"The twins have school," she pointed out.

"There is this thing called home schooling," I said.

Aidan looked at me. "You'd be on board with that?"

"Sure, why not? The kids get to run around on the beach. I'd prefer if they were outside getting sun and exercise. Who knows, I might actually be able to tan if were here long enough."

Annie's eyes widened. "You're serious about this."

The lights in the kitchen flickered.

Aidan grinned. "Ray likes our plan."

"Oh stop," Annie muttered. "That's not confirmation. This is insanity."

"The best things are," Caleb said.

"What about my jam business?" Annie demanded.

"You were going to hire help," Caleb said. "And you're bored with it already. How many days can you keep making the same jam over and over before you're ready for a new challenge? Hire someone to make your recipes in bulk and package everything and spend your time doing this."

She held up her hand in the universal symbol of needing a minute. "I just can't with this right now."

"Annie," Caleb began.

"No, I—let me have some space."

He nodded slowly.

Annie stomped out the back door which then shut with a resounding thud. It was just the three of us.

"I'm giving her five minutes," Caleb said. "And then I'm going to intrude on her space."

"Daddy!" Matilda yelled, the sound traveling all the way from upstairs.

Caleb sighed.

"I'll go talk to Annie. If you're cool with that?" I said to him.

"Please."

I took to the beach. The sound of the waves was soothing and the sun was warm on my neck.

Annie was sitting on the sand, her fingers sifting through granules. She looked forlornly out to the horizon, appearing as lost as a ship at sea.

"I know you asked for space, but I'm ignoring you."

She smiled slightly. "I thought it would be Caleb who'd come here."

"Matilda."

"Ah." She nodded.

"Well?" I prodded.

"Well, what?"

"Well, tell me what's on your mind."

"I'm scared."

"Of what? Life changing? I thought we put all that to rest."

"We did," she admitted. "I just—what if this pregnancy is as hard on me as the last one."

"What if it's not?"

"What if I have to be on bed rest?"

"Then you'll have to be on bed rest." I shrugged. "You're not alone. You realize that, right?"

"I know."

"Do you? I mean, do you really know it? You're not like, scared of this endeavor, are you?"

"Nah. I've already opened a restaurant, a jam business, and broke up a wedding to steal back the love of my life. I'm pretty sure I can handle a pizza joint." She looked at me. "How are you so Zen about this? You're not concerned about logistics?"

"Well, let's see… we are all business owners with tons of experience, we've got the funding, and we just happen to have a house that's big enough for all of us to stay in while we get things off the ground. I mean, the haunted thing needs to be addressed, but aside from that? I don't know, it just seems like it's going to work? Besides, I like that we do things together. I like that we're family."

She leaned her head on my shoulder and sighed. "I don't know what I'd do without you."

Chapter 19

"Where are you going?" Aidan asked the moment I climbed out of bed.

"Sorry, did I wake you?"

"No," he mumbled, sounding like his face was still pressed into a pillow. "So where are you going?"

"I can't sleep. I was going to make tea."

"Do you want company?" he asked as he stifled a yawn.

I smiled. "No. You go back to bed."

I leaned over and kissed him. He was already breathing deeply by the time I made it to the door, which I closed quietly behind me.

Instead of heading down to the kitchen, I decided to go to the attic. There were still so many things cluttering the room, despite Jolie's help. The floppy hat and boa sat in a box and I put them on.

A red-handled piece of luggage was underneath a stack of boxes. It intrigued me. I moved things aside and pulled out the carrying case.

I unlatched it and lifted the lid and gasped.

A vintage mint green Smith-Corono typewriter sat before me.

I punched a key, loving the sound. It echoed through the room. There was a stack of paper underneath the type-writer. I took a piece and fed it into the machine. I pressed the R button. Ink stamped the paper.

And in solitude by the orange glow of an old attic light in the middle of the night, I began to tell a story.

Something warm and wet touched my face. Wrinkling my nose, I batted at my cheek.

And came in direct contact with fur.

I opened one eye and let out a squeak.

A scraggly white and gray kitten was nuzzling against me and licking me with a tiny pink tongue.

Once my heart rate returned to normal, I let out a sigh of relief. Thank God it hadn't been a rat. Or a possum.

"How did you get in here?" The little beast jumped down from my shoulder to the floor. It looked up at me with beggar's eyes.

"I don't know anything about cats," I said to it. "Are you sure you want to stay here?"

It meowed.

I sighed. "Are you hungry? I'm hungry."

My tailbone was numb, and my eyes were gritty. I glanced down at the typewriter and the pages and pages of story I had. I quickly maneuvered the typewriter and paper into the corner and out of sight.

"Ready?" I asked the kitten.

It cocked its head to the side, like it was debating.

"I've got anchovies," I offered.

It leapt forward and dogged my heels all the way down the stairs, through the hallway, and into the kitchen.

Haha. Dogged.

Annie was already awake, sitting at the kitchen table with Matilda who was eating oatmeal and making a complete mess of it.

"Hello, Dolly," Annie said.

"Huh?"

She gestured to my head.

"I'm wearing a hat," I commented.

"And a boa."

"I forgot. I fell asleep in the attic."

"Why did you fall asleep in the attic?"

"I couldn't sleep, so I went up and started going through boxes." It wasn't the entire truth, but I wasn't ready to tell anyone about the story that I'd started writing. No outline, no plot, just words on a page that wanted to come out.

"Meow!"

"That's a kitty!" Matilda shrieked.

"Kitty?" Annie asked in confusion.

"A rogue kitten found its way into the attic and woke me up." I leaned down and scooped up the cat and all but shoved it in Annie's face.

"It looks young," she said.

"And hungry. I can see its ribs sticking out."

"I want it!" Matilda yelled.

"The cat needs to see a vet," I said. "And it needs anchovies. I promised it anchovies."

"Why didn't you promise it tuna?"

"Because we have anchovies in the cupboard. I have no idea what to do with this cat."

"Keep it?"

"What about Jasper?" I asked.

"I'm sure Jasper would love a companion."

"What about Aidan?"

"What about Aidan what?" my husband asked.

I turned and held up the kitten. "Can we keep it?"

"This was not part of the plan," I said from the passenger side of the pink Cadillac.

Aidan grinned. "Have we ever had a plan?"

"Good point."

We were driving home from the vet with the newest member of our family. The kitten was a female. She was about six weeks old, and she'd been dewormed and had a complete checkup and a few shots.

"What should we name her?" I asked. The kitten was currently asleep, nestled underneath my shirt against my skin purring softy. She was quickly turning me into a cat person.

"I think we should let the kids name her," Aidan said.

"Fantastic idea. Oh, turn here!"

"Why?" he asked even as he did as I said.

"Because three blocks away there's an adorable little drive thru with ice cream, hot dogs, and milk shakes. And I want to take you to lunch."

"I thought you said Bob's was the only food place in town."

"This place is technically not within town limits," I explained. "Jolie and I found it while we were off exploring the area."

Once we had our burgers and fries, we parked in a lot underneath a shady tree and devoured our lunch. The kitten popped her head out of my shirt, and I fed her a fry.

"Jasper is going to be insanely jealous," Aidan said.

"Why? I always share my fries with him." I gave the kitten another French fry and to thank me, she nuzzled her head against my neck. "I miss him."

"Yeah, I know I was supposed to drive down with him, but I wanted to get to Gator Springs ASAP. I could always fly back up there and then road trip down."

"It's a lot of traveling for you, but I want our entire family together, and that includes Jasper."

"Then I'll do it. We need the Subaru anyway for when we drive home." Aidan whipped out his cell phone. "Let's call the kids."

Sophie answered her grandfather's cell phone on the first ring. "I haven't pooped today," she informed us.

"No?" I asked.

"Two words," came Nancy's voice from somewhere in the background. "Onion Brick."

"Oh no," I said. "We forgot to warn you. Never let Sophie have an Onion Brick."

"Oliver tried to warn us," Nancy said. "But then Sophie promised to marry the server if he brought her one. He couldn't resist her."

"You're far too charming for your own good," I said to Sophie.

Sophie grinned. "I get it from Dad."

"What do you get from me?"

"My sense of humor."

Well, she had me there.

"We have a surprise for you and Ollie," Aidan said. "Where's your brother?"

"Trying to find something fun to watch on TV. There's never anything on," Sophie said.

"Get him, will you?"

"K," she said. "Ollie! Mom and Dad are on the phone! And they have a surprise!"

Oliver suddenly appeared next to his sister. His hair was askew when normally it was combed to perfection.

"What happened to your hair?" I asked.

"Ashley likes it messed up. So I'm wearing it this way."

"It looks nice," I said, wishing my son wasn't suddenly obsessed with impressing the opposite sex.

"So, what's the surprise?" Oliver asked. "Do I get a brother?"

I frowned. "Why do you need a brother? You have a sister."

"Yeah," Sophie said, putting her hands on her hips and looking at him. "You have a sister."

"But a brother would be nice," Oliver said.

"You're not getting a brother," I said, stopping the fight brewing between the twins. "But you are getting a kitten!"

I lifted the cat to the screen.

Sophie jumped around in excitement, but Oliver didn't look at all impressed. "We have a dog," he said.

"Yes," I agreed.

"I don't want a cat," Oliver said.

"I want a cat!" Sophie squealed.

"You guys want to name her?" Aidan asked, ignoring Oliver's lack of enthusiasm.

"Sophie can do it," Oliver said and then he walked away.

I looked at Aidan and raised my brows. Had our son skipped the normal years and gone straight to moody teen?

Aidan shrugged.

"Okay, Soph, what do you want to name her?" I asked.

"Lady Fluffalump, but we can call her Fluffy."

"She's so your daughter," Aidan said under his breath.

"Lady Fluffalump it is," I said. "What color collar do you want for her?"

"Purple."

"Like Roman royalty," Aidan quipped.

Sophie scrunched her nose. "Huh?"

"Never mind," Aidan said.

My phone started buzzing in my lap and I looked at the screen. "Sophie, we gotta go. We'll call you later."

"Send me videos of Lady Fluffalump!" Sophie said and then she hung up.

I picked up my phone and answered it. "Mom? Hi."

"Hi," she greeted. "I just wanted to let you know that we're on the road. We should be there by dinnertime."

"Excellent," I said. "Any dinner preferences?"

"Whatever's easiest."

"That's very go with the flow of you, Mom."

"It's the only way to be these days. Keeps the blood pressure down. So does cannabis."

"Excuse me?"

"Marijuana, Sibby. Specifically, edibles."

"What kind of luncheons are you attending these days?" I demanded.

She giggled.

Actually *giggled*.

"Your father's driving, so don't worry about a thing. See you in a few hours!"

"Meow!"

"You don't have to meow at me," she sniffed.

"I didn't meow at you," I said in exasperation. "My cat did."

"You have a cat? When did you get a cat?"

"Last night. A kitten was in the attic and claimed me for its own. Sophie named her Lady Fluffalump."

"Hmm, that's nice. Well, the traffic is getting a bit heavy, so I better sign off. See you soon!"

She hung up and I looked at Aidan. "Did you hear any of that?"

"I heard all of it. Your mother is into edibles now, huh?"

"Apparently." I grinned. "She's becoming really fun."

"Let's run to the pet store, get Lady Fluffalump a collar and some food, and then I'll help with the doll room."

"You just said Lady Fluffalump with a straight face. You just became a cat guy."

Chapter 20

"No. You can't. You can't keep that doll."

Lady Fluffalump looked up with sweet brown eyes as she pawed at the face of the china doll that looked like it was about to die of Scarlet Fever.

"It's terrifying," I said.

She meowed.

I sighed. "Jasper will not be as easy to manipulate, I assure you. If you attempt to steal his hedgehog squeaker toy, he'll put you in your place."

She nosed the creepy doll and then began to purr.

"I've gotten soft in my old age," I muttered.

"You talk to yourself more now, too."

"Gah!" I whirled to find Aidan smiling at me from the doorway of the china doll room.

"I got a case of wine," he said. "You think that's enough?"

"Uh. Yeah. My mom's a light weight. And who knows if she even drinks now that she's discovered edibles."

"I figured we could bring a bunch to Betty Sue's party."

"Good plan."

"Lady Fluffalump has made herself at home on that doll. Why does it look like it's dying?"

"No idea." I shuddered. "Will you help me cart these boxes up to the attic?"

"I thought the purpose of cleaning out the attic was not to bring more stuff up there."

"I don't know what to do with these dolls. There's not like a creepy doll museum in town, and I don't want to see the boxes which will remind me of what's in them. Plus, the humidity might ruin them if I leave them on the porch."

"Up to the attic we go," he said, grabbing a box. I followed behind him with another. "Where do you want them?"

"Far corner," I said when we got up to the attic.

"Out of sight out of mind." He set the box down in the corner and then took the other box from me, setting it on top of the other.

His eyes roamed over the room. "I thought you said you and Jolie made progress going through stuff."

"Uh, we did make progress. For the record we didn't find a treasure map on the back of a painting."

"Sad."

"Very," I agreed.

"What's that?"

"What's what?"

He pointed to the typewriter. "That."

"Oh, it's…a typewriter."

"Obviously," he said. "I meant the stack of papers next to it. It looks like a manuscript. Was Aunt Ida writing an autobiography?"

I paused. "Actually, that's mine."

"Yours? You're writing an autobiography?"

"No. But I am writing…something. Last night when you went back to bed, I came up here and found the typewriter and then just started typing away."

"You did?"

I nodded.

"Is it a romance?"

"It might be a romance," I said with a small smile. "It's too soon to tell."

He wrapped his arm around my shoulder and pulled me into his chest. "Looks like you made decent progress."

"Chipping away at it." I looked at it forlornly.

"You can't stop thinking about it, can you?"

I bit my lip. "No, I can't."

"Then get back to it."

"I can't. My parents will be here soon."

"I'll come get you when they show up. Take some time up here if that's what you want."

I shook my head, a smile playing on my lips.

"What?" he asked.

"You. You just—yeah."

"I love you too."

"Thanks for getting me."

He leaned down and kissed my lips. "Ditto."

The sound of laughter pulled me from the story. I had no idea the time since I'd left my cell phone in the bedroom so I wouldn't get distracted.

There was something deeply fulfilling using a type-writer instead of a computer. There were no distractions. My fingers couldn't keep up with my brain, forcing me to slow down. I had to think as I punched the keys, so I was typing out fully formed ideas.

I stood up and groaned. I'd been hunched over and cross-legged. Dehydrated and hungry, I trekked downstairs into the kitchen.

The sight that greeted me warmed my heart. My mother was standing next to Annie holding a glass of wine. Annie had Matilda to her hip and my mother reached out to slide a strand of hair behind the little girl's ear. My father was conversing with Caleb and Aidan, his bushy eyebrows rising to his hair line and then his booming laughter echoing around the room.

Several eight-inch pizzas graced the table and my stomach rumbled in excitement and eagerness. Some of them were already half eaten.

I looked at Annie and raised my brows. She shrugged and then grinned. "Recipe testing."

"I figured."

Aidan saw me out of the corner of his eye and turned his body toward me. "The reclusive writer has emerged."

I smiled. "She has emerged with a hungry demon in her belly." I approached my mother first and gave her a strong hug. "I'm glad you're here."

She squeezed me back with one arm. "This house is incredible. I had no idea."

"Annie gave you the tour?" I asked.

"She did. She showed us the guest bedroom and the

kitten that is currently curled up against the pillows, purring on a china doll."

"Isn't she adorable?"

"Completely. I might stick her in my purse and steal her when you're not looking."

"Sophie has already seen her and will go positively feral on you. You've been warned."

Mom touched my cheek and then hugged me again. "You look good."

"Do I?"

"Yes."

"Even with the frizzy hair?"

"I think it adds a certain appeal."

My mother was a tinier, more put together version of me. She was the OG when it came to dramatics and theatrics, but her heart was made of gold.

"What, you ignore me completely?" my dad said.

Mom let me go and I cuddled against my father's chest like Lady Fluffalump did to me. There was something so strong and reassuring about a father's hug. Even as an adult, I still felt like he could slay the monsters under my bed.

"You look tan," I said to him as I pulled back.

"I spend five days a week on the golf course," he reminded me.

"Hmm, that'll do it."

Annie handed me a glass of red wine, which I took with gratitude.

"Aidan said you were writing in the attic?" Dad asked.

"Aunt Ida had a vintage typewriter that I found and it's in great condition. I've been using that since my computer went on the fritz."

Dad grinned. "Another one? What happened this time?"

"You think I know?" I shook my head. "I sent it off to the kind computer people who know me by first name. Hopefully they can save it."

Annie offered me an empty plate. "Hope you don't mind, but we dove in without you. Your mother couldn't wait."

"My mother couldn't wait," I repeated. "That doesn't sound like her. She's not driven by food."

"What's she driven by?"

"Sephora products." I frowned and then suddenly I was smiling ear to ear.

"What?" Annie asked. "What's that grin for?"

I leaned in and whispered, "My mom discovered edibles."

"No." Annie gasped.

"Yes."

"Oh my God, that makes me love her even more. What about your Dad?"

"What about him?"

"Do you think he's partaking in edibles, too?"

I glanced at my father. "I don't know. He plays golf and drinks scotch. I'm pretty sure that's as rowdy as he gets."

"I love your parents," Annie said with a sigh. "I really do."

Mom and I left everyone sitting around the bonfire to walk down to the surf. It was a cloudy night and it was difficult to see, so we didn't go far.

"I spoke with *Bubbe* this morning," Mom said as the ocean swirled around our ankles.

"Yeah?"

"They've docked for a few days and she was able to call. So, I asked her about Aunt Ida's past relationships. Ray was the love of her life. They met when she was galivanting across Spain in the seventies. They fell in love quickly and passionately. He died two years later of cancer. They never got married."

"That's sad," I said. "Really sad."

"Maybe."

Mom peered up at the stars and fell silent.

"What do you mean, maybe? She found the love of her life and he died shortly after they met."

"Yes, but they met. What if they'd never met at all?"

"I didn't think of that."

She looked at me. "Annie's pregnant, hmm?"

"How did you—they weren't planning on telling anyone for a few weeks."

"Oh, please. She's so easy to read. So, a pizza and beer place in Gator Springs."

"Yeah."

"You kids and all your energy." She shook her head. "I'm proud of you, you know. You dive into life, and I think that's wonderful."

"Thanks, Mom," I said, tears filling my eyes.

"What's this new book about?"

"Not sure yet. I'm just letting the words carry the story. No pressure. But I'm enjoying it."

"I know whatever you write will be amazing. I believe in you, Sibby. I always have."

Chapter 21

"Who is this woman?" Mom asked as the group of us trekked up the walkway to Betty Sue's front porch.

"Betty Sue," I said. "She was the one who wanted to buy Aunt Ida's place and turn it into a bed and breakfast."

"She's also the one that tipped off the sheriff and had him run the plates on the beater car that Jolie didn't know was stolen," Annie piped up.

"So she's the enemy?" Mom asked, her expression darkening.

"Stand down, woman," I said. "We've come to an understanding. She's throwing this party as an apology, but also as a welcome to the community now that we've made it clear we're keeping Aunt Ida's place."

"I'll ensure your mother is on her best behavior," Dad said, taking Mom's hand and giving it a squeeze.

"Give her an edible," Annie muttered. "It'll calm her down."

"I heard that," Mom said.

I rang the bell and a moment later, the door opened. Betty Sue stood on the threshold, looking like she'd stepped out of a time machine. Her dress was cherry-print, and her eyebrows were drawn on her face.

"Oh my," Mom said.

"Sibby!" Betty Sue greeted. "Come in, come in."

Her home was immaculate and warm. She was just the sort of person who would successfully run a bed and breakfast. I almost regretted not selling Ida's home to her.

Almost.

"Who is this?" Betty Sue asked with a smile at Matilda who was shyly peering at Betty Sue from the crook of Caleb's neck.

"This is Matilda," Annie said.

"She's precious," Betty Sue said. She then looked at the box in Aidan's arms. "What did you bring?"

"Wine," Aidan announced. "You can never have too much wine."

We moved farther into the house that was already full of people standing in the living room and kitchen, holding drinks. Platters of food graced the counter tops and table.

"Norm and the boys are outside," Betty Sue said to Aidan. "Norm hasn't been able to stop talking about you."

"I made an impression, did I?"

"You did." Betty Sue turned her attention to my parents, and I quickly made the introductions.

Mom melted under Betty Sue's enthusiasm, and soon they were linked, arm in arm with Betty Sue taking my mother around to meet everyone.

"Well, Dad," I said. "You can either hang out with me or you can go talk with Aidan and Norm about hunting swamp rats."

"I'll stick close to you," he said with a grin. "I don't know nothin' about huntin' swamp rats."

"Neither does Aidan, but he seems intrigued."

Ellie and Ralph stood in the corner of the living

room, absorbed in conversation. Ellie's cheeks were flushed and Ralph looked eager as he inched closer to her.

"I need a drink," Dad said.

"Me too," Caleb said.

"Let's go," Dad said.

"I thought you were sticking close to me?" I raised my brows.

"I'll return, I promise."

"Annie?" Caleb asked.

"Club soda or water, please." She held out her hands to Matilda who went willingly to her mother.

My father and Caleb wandered in the direction of the kitchen, leaving me alone with Annie.

The doorbell rang and when Betty Sue didn't run to answer it, I took it upon myself to do so. Jolie and Luke stood at the threshold, looking cute and coupley.

"Why are you answering the door?" Jolie asked.

"Because Betty Sue is obsessed with my mother. They're making the rounds."

"Oh sure," Jolie said, coming into the house. Her blonde hair was down and it was stick straight.

She did not suffer from Jewmidity, darn her.

"Hey, Luke," I said with a smile.

"Hi," he greeted. "I haven't eaten yet and I'm starving. Someone point me in the direction of the food."

I pointed toward the kitchen.

"Need anything?" Luke asked, looking at Jolie.

She shook her head.

"I'll go with you," Annie offered. "I'm starving too."

Luke kissed Jolie's cheek and then Luke and Annie went toward the buffet.

It was like the house swallowed up the people from my entourage.

"My mom talked to my grandmother and found out about Ray," I said to Jolie.

"No way! Who is he?"

"The love of Ida's life." I quickly explained what my mom had shared with me.

"It would make for a good book and a great adaptation into a movie," Jolie said, elbowing me in the side. "I've got some news."

"The charges have been dropped?" I asked hopefully.

"Not yet. Soon," she assured me. "I bought a house down here."

"What?" I asked in shock. "You didn't."

"I did."

"But why? You didn't buy a house down here because of the criminal charges, did you? You can stay with us until—"

"No. That's not why I bought the house. It's just a tiny little thing. A cottage really. Quaint, under the radar. The window AC unit doesn't even work half the time. It's perfect."

"I don't understand."

"Well, criminal charges or no criminal charges, I've decided to take a step back from the limelight for a bit, and I wanted to be comfortable. And I really like it here."

"How does Luke feel about you buying the house?" I asked her with a smile.

"I haven't told him yet. I wanted it to be a surprise."

"He'll definitely be surprised."

"Who will be surprised?" Luke asked, returning to the foyer where Jolie and I were still currently standing.

"You," Jolie said. "When I tell you I bought a house in Gator Springs."

His eyes widened. "You didn't—I mean—not because of me?"

She snorted. "Do I have stage 5 clinger written on my forehead? No. I didn't buy the house because of you. I bought it for several reasons. I plan on staying in the area for a little while."

"Oh, well, that's good. I mean, if you had bought the house because of me, that would've been…"

Jolie arched an eyebrow. "Would've been what?"

The front door crashed open and a tall, burly, dark-haired man stood in the doorframe. His hair was askew, and his brown eyes were wild. His navy-blue button down was rolled up to reveal sleeves of tattoos and his beard was bushy but well-kept.

The man looked right at Jolie and an audible gasp escaped her lips. "Hamish? What are you doing here?"

"Hamish?" I repeated. "Hamish McTiernan? The co-star who you…"

Jolie nodded distractedly, her eyes still on Hamish.

"You're letting in the mosquitoes," Jolie said faintly.

Hamish stepped inside and closed the door.

"What are you doing here?" she demanded again.

"Looking for you," he said, his silky voice spilling out of his mouth. The jerk even had an Irish accent that dripped with sensuality.

No wonder she'd slept with him.

"Who was at the door?" came Betty Sue's question.

"Er, uh," I began.

"I need to speak with you. Now," Hamish commanded.

Luke slid to Jolie's side, but he didn't say anything, he merely gave Jolie his solidarity.

"We have nothing to say to one another," Jolie said. "I'm at a party. And you can show yourself out. I told you to stop calling me."

I looked at her. "He's been calling you?"

She nodded.

"For how long?"

"Since I got here," she explained.

"You wouldn't call me back, so I had to show up," Hamish said.

"Stalker alert," Annie said, coming to stand on my other side.

I looked behind me to see my parents, Caleb, and even Betty Sue. I couldn't help the smile from stretching across my face.

"I'm not a stalker, I just…" Hamish ran a hand through his hair, making it stand on end. "Can we please go somewhere to talk?"

"No." Jolie tossed her head and crossed her arms over her chest. "Whatever you want to say, you can say it front of them."

"This is private," Hamish said.

"Goodbye, Hamish." She waved.

"It was a publicity stunt," he blurted out. "My wife and I really are separated, and my agent thought this would help revitalize my career. I'm gonna need the money after the divorce. Alimony is a bitch."

"*Revitalize your career?*" Jolie screeched. "My reputation is in the toilet because your agent is an *asshole*?"

"I fired him. If that makes you feel any better."

"No. It doesn't. It doesn't undo the damage. I haven't heard you releasing a statement, absolving me of home-wrecking your marriage when it was already wrecked!"

"I'm releasing a statement in a few days. I've talked to the producers of the show. They're going to reach out and ask you to come back."

"They killed off my character!" she yelled.

"Hey!" I scowled. "I haven't watched it yet."

Jolie looked at me and glared.

"Oh, right. Bigger issues," I said. "Sorry."

"I'm in love with you," Hamish stated.

Someone's breath hitched, but I had no idea who it was.

"I'm in love with you," Hamish went on. "And I'll do anything to get you back."

"There is no *back*," Jolie stated. "There was no front."

"That didn't make sense," my mother murmured.

"She meant that she was never truly with Hamish," I said with a look at Jolie. "Right?"

"Right," she agreed with a nod.

I glanced at Luke whose body was taut with tension. His fists were clenched, and he looked ready to throw down.

Jolie caught sight of Luke and immediately placed a hand on his chest. I watched Hamish's expression tighten and then his jaw clamped shut.

"Okay, this has been super fun," I said awkwardly, "thanks for stopping by Hamish, but I think it's time for you to go."

"Past time," Aidan voiced.

There was a rumble of agreement in the room.

Hamish knew he was defeated, and even though he looked like he wanted a fight, he didn't pursue it.

"Call me," he said to Jolie. "Please."

He didn't wait for her to reply. Hamish slipped through the door and was gone.

No one said anything for a very long time, until finally, Ralph said, "Things here have never been this interesting."

Jolie stared at Luke. "Can we talk?"

Luke nodded. "Let's go."

Jolie turned and addressed the small group of people who'd literally stood behind her. "Thank you. All of you."

"We didn't get a chance to talk," Mom said. "You'll come to breakfast at the house tomorrow?"

Jolie cracked a smile of relief. "Yeah, I will."

Mom looked at Luke. "You too."

"Yes, ma'am," Luke stated.

He ushered Jolie out of the house.

"How does it feel?" Aidan asked.

"How does what feel?" I repeated.

"Not to be the cause of the drama for once."

"Honestly? I'm not really sure. Drama is part of my identity and now I feel kind of lost."

An hour later, Annie pulled me aside and said, "We're going to go."

"Go? Why? It's only eight o'clock," I protested.

Jolie and Luke hadn't returned, and the party guests were slowly dwindling. It wasn't really a late-night crowd in Gator Springs.

"I'm not feeling great," she admitted. "I'm kinda nauseous and clammy. It's the pregnancy thing."

"Right. The pregnancy thing. I knew that."

Annie grinned. "You're a little tipsy."

"Maybe just a little."

"Good, you deserve to let loose a bit." She hugged me.

"I'll probably be asleep by the time you guys get back, so I'll say goodnight now."

"Good night."

"Your mom is in rare form," she said with a smile and a chin nod in the direction of my mother, who was kibbitzing with Ellie and the other salon gals.

"You know what I think?" I asked.

"What?"

"This town is pretty charming."

"It is, isn't it?"

"What do you think is happening between Jolie and Luke?" she asked.

"The horizontal hora."

"Really?"

"Yup. He's committed. I can tell. She bought a house down here."

"Get out!"

"She just told me."

"Ready to go?" Caleb asked, sidling up next to Annie with a sleeping Matilda against his shoulder.

"I'm ready." To me she said, "There's still a few pieces of pizza left over in the fridge for when you need a snack."

"You take such good care of me."

"Someone has to."

"If it weren't for you, I would never eat a vegetable."

"Same," Caleb voiced.

Aidan came up and wrapped his arms around me from behind. "Can we get out of here?"

"Really?" I asked, peering up at him. "It's still early."

He whispered in my ear. "Exactly."

I grinned. "What are we waiting for?"

Lady Fluffalump padded around the coverlet before jumping onto Aidan's chest where she curled up and went to sleep.

Aidan looked down at the kitten. "How? How did I become a cat person?"

"You? I considered putting her in my purse to bring her to the party."

"Hey, so guess what?" he asked.

"Chicken butt," I blurted out. "Sorry, old habits. You were saying?"

"One of the bartenders has family in Gainesville and he's taking some time off in about a week. I was thinking he could get the car and drive down with Jasper. With the kids coming in a few days—"

"The kids?" I asked. "The kids are coming in a few days? Why didn't I know about this?"

"Ah, my parents called while we were at the party. The RV is going to take a few weeks to fix, so they're driving the car they were towing behind the RV to Gator Springs."

"Oh man! They have to abandon their national park trip? Major bummer."

"Don't lie, you miss the kids."

"So much," I admitted. "I enjoyed having a little time to myself, but yeah, I miss their crazy."

"Crazy. Yeah, it's always so crazy." He stroked Lady Fluffalump's head. "You doing okay?"

"Me?" I paused and thought for a moment. "Yeah, I'm good."

"Really?" He reached out to touch my leg. "I worry about you."

"You do?"

"Yeah. I want to make sure you're getting what you need."

I arched a brow.

"I didn't mean for that to sound dirty," he said with a grin.

I flopped down next to him and placed my head in the crook where his chest met his arm. I lightly stroked Lady Fluffalump's head. "I have some ideas about some things. They're churning around, but I'm not ready to talk about them. Is that okay?"

"Tell me when you're ready."

"It doesn't bug you? That I'm not confiding in you?"

"No. It doesn't bug me."

"I think about you all the time, you know."

"Yeah?"

"Yeah. I think about everything we've been through, everything we've built, the kids, the businesses. I love you now more than when we met, and I couldn't imagine my life without you."

His arm tightened around me.

"Where are we going to put the kids? There aren't enough rooms," I said in realization. "Where are we going to put your parents? We could give them the master bedroom if we clean out the attic and stick trundle beds up there. Then you, me, and the kids can camp out."

"But that's where you've been writing," he said.

"Yes."

"I don't want you to have to sacrifice a quiet space. You need a writing den."

"We could fit a teeny tiny desk in the corner of the attic," I suggested. "That's all I really need."

"Hmm," Aidan murmured.

I perked my head up to look at him. His eyes were closed, and the kitten was purring. I gently rolled out of his arms and turned off the lamp light before padding from the room.

The house was quiet despite it being a relatively early hour. I headed downstairs, not yet ready to go to sleep. My mother was in the kitchen, putting on water for tea.

"Hey," I said.

"Hey. That was a fun party."

"It was."

"A lot of excitement. Jolie's life is like a movie."

"Yeah, it is, isn't it?" I smiled. "Mom?"

"Yes?"

"Can I ask you a favor?"

"Sure."

"Will you take a walk with me along the beach?"

"Now?"

I nodded.

"Everything okay?"

"Everything's fine. I just—Aunt Ida was cremated," I said. "I wasn't sure what to do with her ashes, but I am now."

"The ocean?"

"Yes. She loved it here."

"She did. Everyone at the party had the loveliest things to say about her. I wish I'd known her better."

"Me too," I said.

I went in the living room and Mom followed me. I grasped the box of ashes off the mantle.

"There are other boxes," Mom commented.

"Her furry companions."

"Ah."

"I think we should spread their ashes too. I think she'd want them with her. Is that weird? That sounds weird."

"I think it sounds thoughtful." Mom took the other boxes and we tromped out into the night. We kicked off our sandals and stood in the surf as we spread Aunt Ida's ashes underneath the moon and starlight.

The sound of the waves hit my ears. Mom and I stood arm in arm, silent, looking up at the sky.

"Life's pretty wonderful, isn't it?" I asked her.

"Yeah, Sibby. It is."

Epilogue

Two weeks later

JASPER BARKED as he chased the twins across the sand. Aidan's parents and mine sat underneath the beach umbrella while they kept an eye on Matilda.

"I think this is the best summer I've ever had," Annie said from behind large sunglasses.

"Same," Jolie commented. She wore a big floppy hat

that kept the sun off her face. Luke grasped her hand and brought it to his lips.

"What about you, Sib?" Aidan asked. "How's this summer ranking in all of the summers thus far?"

"I had a really fun summer when I was twelve and I got to go to camp. But this is a solid contender," I said.

"Ah, camp," Annie said with a sigh. "I got into so much trouble at camp."

"Oh yeah?" Caleb asked his wife. "What kind of trouble."

"Like sneaking out of my bunk to meet a boy by the lake kind of trouble." Annie grinned. "He wasn't a good kisser, though. You're much better."

"So glad to hear it," Caleb remarked dryly.

"Did you guys hear that a building on Main Street is going up for sale in the next few weeks?" Luke asked.

"Norm told me," Aidan said. "We've already got a meeting with the owner to make an offer."

"I can't believe you guys are doing this," Jolie said. "A pizza and beer joint. Genius."

"We'll see," Caleb said. "But we're all pretty hopeful."

"With a celebrity that's moved to Gator Springs I anticipate some more traffic," I said. "Can't exactly build a business on a couple hundred locals in their seventies."

The criminal charges had been dropped, but Jolie still wasn't going to back to the show. Despite the fact that the producers had offered her more money and the writers had had a plan to bring her back from the dead, she'd walked away.

"I think I'm ready for a nap," Annie said. "And I want to get out of the sun."

"Matilda needs a nap, too," Caleb said.

"We should run to the store," Luke said to Jolie. "And grab the burgers and hotdogs to grill for tonight."

"And get the fixings for potato salad," Annie said.

"Oh yes, she makes a killer potato salad," I added.

"I don't know what's in a potato salad," Jolie said with a frown.

"Potatoes, obviously," I quipped.

She stuck her tongue out at me.

"I'll give you a list of ingredients," Annie said.

After Caleb scooped up Matilda from the sand, the four of them trekked toward the house and disappeared.

I took Aidan's hand and said, "I'm ready to tell you what I've been noodling over."

"Oh yeah?"

"Yeah." I nodded. "This house is an amazing gift. Truly wonderful, but it's a shame for it to stand empty half the year."

"I agree," he said.

"Now that Ray moved along and is now with Ida," I smiled at him. "I want to open the house up to other writers. I want it to be a place for them to come and clear their heads and type on typewriters. To brainstorm, to dream, to let the words flow from their fingertips. I want to give something back, Aidan. I want to bring a community of writers together so we can share and grow and support one another. I didn't know how much I needed that until I realized that I don't have that. So I want to create it."

"You want to host writer's retreats," he stated. "Is that what you're telling me?"

"Yeah, that's what I'm telling you."

He turned me to him and stared at me. And then he smiled. The smile lines around his eyes were more pronounced. Aidan spent so much of his time smiling.

"You always surprise me, Sibby," he said.

"I do?"

He nodded. "Yeah. You inspire me. Do you know that?"

"Really?"

"Yes. I'm so proud of you."

I sighed. "I can do anything, with you by my side. I can't thank you enough."

"For what?"

"For being my partner. For being my husband. For being the father to my children. For never laughing at my dreams."

He cradled my cheeks in his hands and brought his lips to mine. "We're in this wild ride together."

"Until the bitter end?" I teased.

"Nothing bitter about it, Sib. Nothing bitter about it."

And with the sound of our children's laughter in our ears, the waves splashing up to our ankles, Aidan kissed me.

It was just like the first time. Only better. Because it was forever.

About the Author

Wall Street Journal & *USA Today* bestselling author Emma Slate writes romance with heart and heat.

Called "the dialogue queen" by her college playwriting professor, Emma writes love stories that range from romance-for-your-pants to action-flicks-for-chicks.

When she isn't writing, she's usually curled up under a heating blanket with a steamy romance novel and her two beagles—unless her outdoorsy husband can convince her to go on a hike.

Emma also writes rom-com and contemporary romance as E. Slate.

____

Additional Works

____

<u>Writing as E. Slate</u>

The Sibby Series

Queen of Klutz (Book 1)
Sibby Slicker (Book 2)
Mother Shucker (Book 3)
Sibby's Spawn (Book 4)
Hot Mess Express (Book 5)

Others:

From Stardust to Stardust

<u>Writing as Emma Slate</u>

The Tarnished Angels Motorcycle Club Series:

Wreck & Ruin (Tarnished Angels Book 1)
Crash & Carnage (Tarnished Angels Book 2)

Madness & Mayhem (Tarnished Angels Book 3)
Thrust & Throttle (Tarnished Angels Book 4)
Venom & Vengeance (Tarnished Angels Book 5)
Fire & Frenzy (Tarnished Angels Book 6)
Leather & Lies (Tarnished Angels Book 7)
Heartbeats & Highways (Tarnished Angels Book 8)

SINS Series:

Sins of a King (Book 1)
Birth of a Queen (Book 2)
Rise of a Dynasty (Book 3)
Dawn of an Empire (Book 4)
Ember (Book 5)
Burn (Book 6)
Ashes (Book 7)
Fall of a Kingdom (Book 8)

Others:

Peasants and Kings

www.ingramcontent.com/pod-product-compliance
Lightning Source LLC
Chambersburg PA
CBHW032221190726
48289CB00007BA/2333